"I'd Like You To Come Home With Me And Pretend You Love Me."

Zack had heard all kinds of propositions throughout the course of his career. Not a one had the nuclear-bomb effect of this particular one.

"You want to take me home?" he asked stupidly. Then, a bit louder, "And pretend I love you? Is that what you said?"

"Well, don't look so shocked," Anna said. "You won't be in any mortal danger or anything. The key to the whole thing is *pretend*. For heaven's sake, you're a cop. I thought you were used to unusual situations." Then, after a short pause, "You've never been this quiet for this long. Are you still breathing?"

Zack realized he wasn't, and immediately rectified the matter. "I'm not shocked," he gasped, pulling oxygen into his paralyzed lungs. "I've been around, you know. It takes a lot to shock me. It's just…it's just…"

"It's just what?"

I've never had a dream come true before.

Dear Reader,

What could be more satisfying than the sinful yet guilt-free pleasure of enjoying six new passionate, powerful and provocative Silhouette Desire romances this month?

Get started with *In Blackhawk's Bed*, July's MAN OF THE MONTH and the latest title in the SECRETS! miniseries by Barbara McCauley. *The Royal & the Runaway Bride* by Kathryn Jensen—in which the heroine masquerades as a horse trainer and becomes a princess—is the seventh exciting installment in DYNASTIES: THE CONNELLYS, about an American family that discovers its royal roots.

A single mom melts the steely defenses of a brooding ranch hand in *Cowboy's Special Woman* by Sara Orwig, while a detective with a secret falls for an innocent beauty in *The Secret Millionaire* by Ryanne Corey. A CEO persuades a mail-room employee to be his temporary wife in the debut novel *Cinderella & the Playboy* by Laura Wright, praised by *New York Times* bestselling author Debbie Macomber as "a wonderful new voice in Silhouette Desire." And in *Zane: The Wild One* by Bronwyn Jameson, the mayor's daughter turns up the heat on the small town's bad boy made good.

So pamper the romantic in you by reading all six of these great new love stories from Silhouette Desire!

Enjoy!

Joan Marlow Golan

Joan Marlow Golan
Senior Editor, Silhouette Desire

Please address questions and book requests to:
Silhouette Reader Service
U.S.: 3010 Walden Ave., P.O. Box 1325, Buffalo, NY 14269
Canadian: P.O. Box 609, Fort Erie, Ont. L2A 5X3

The Secret Millionaire
RYANNE COREY

Published by Silhouette Books
America's Publisher of Contemporary Romance

SILHOUETTE BOOKS

ISBN 0-373-76450-2

THE SECRET MILLIONAIRE

Copyright © 2002 by Tonya Wood

This edition published by arrangement with Harlequin Books S.A.

® and TM are trademarks of Harlequin Books S.A., used under license.
Trademarks indicated with ® are registered in the United States Patent
and Trademark Office, the Canadian Trade Marks Office and in other
countries.

Visit Silhouette at www.eHarlequin.com

Printed in U.S.A.

RYANNE COREY

is the award-winning author of over twenty romance novels. She is also the recipient of the *Romantic Times* Lifetime Achievement Award. She finds the peace and beauty of the mountains very conducive to writing, and currently lives in the beautiful Rocky Mountains of Utah. She has long believed in the healing power of love and laughter, and enjoys nothing more than bringing a smile to a reader's face.

One

Zack Daniels was an alpha male, from his gleaming ebony hair to the blue-and-white toes of his well-broken-in Reeboks.

He knew this because he watched the Animal Planet channel and was well-informed when it came to the characteristics of a dominant wolf, dog, cheetah, etc. Animal or human, the alpha males were easy to spot. They were driven by their powerful wills, more likely to survive harsh circumstances and always ready for a fight to maintain order in the pack.

True to form, Zack didn't mind the occasional tussle. In fact, at the moment he was absolutely *itching* for a fight. He needed to vent.

He knew with total certainty that he was the most frustrated human being in the state of California. And when he drove his platinum silver 2001 Lotus Esprit across the California border into Oregon, he became the most frustrated human being in Oregon, as well. And why?

Because he was on vacation.

Zack could understand why maybe an accountant or an attorney or a loan officer at a bank would look forward to two weeks of vacation. Those poor guys were stuck in their routines day after day, often glued to a desk and forced to deal with tedious things like billing hours, credit reports and balance sheets. And what did they have to show for their labors at the end of the day? Could they look in a secure jail cell and wave to a dangerous criminal they had personally tracked down and apprehended? They could not. And how many distraught damsels in distress did the poor fellows come across in their line of work? Zack would venture to guess: none. Of course they loved their vacations. They looked forward to having a break from the relentless monotony of their lives.

Zack, on the other hand, had a different situation entirely. He was one of the fortunate few who was lucky enough to have a dream job. He was a cop, and he cheerfully danced with danger and unpredictability for the chance to make a difference in the world. And not just a tame waltz, either; he danced a wild tango with his whole heart and soul. He had never believed in doing anything halfway. Granted, he frequently faced risky situations, but on the whole he relished the satisfaction of being a duly sworn-in representative of justice in a world full of bad guys. He hated to sleep, simply because he might miss a chance to protect, serve, defend, nab evildoers and administer justice. He hated to spend an evening at a high-class restaurant, feeling he was somehow failing to do his job if he turned his pager off for two entire hours. But more than anything, Zack hated taking a meaningless vacation from a life that suited him to a T. And right now he was facing an indefinite period of teeth-grinding, nail-biting, migraine-headache boredom.

He had successfully avoided taking a vacation for the past four years. Unfortunately, a short while ago, he and his partner had been ambushed during a drug bust gone bad.

"Pappy" Merkley was a powerful black man who looked more like a football player than a cop. Zack had always considered his friend and mentor impervious to harm, but this time Pappy had taken two bullets in the chest. It was nip and tuck for a couple of days, but the fifty-year-old veteran was a fighter. It was a good thing, too, because Zack would have called the Almighty on the carpet had an idealistic, gentle giant like Pappy lost his life because of a slimeball drug dealer. Once Pappy was moved out of the ICU, Zack was eager to administer what he termed "legal payback."

Zack had many friends who knew him well. Not one of them wanted to be in the same state when he perceived an injustice and lost his temper. His precinct captain, Benjamin Todd, knew very well that it was only a matter of time until his fiercely loyal wunderkind tracked down the shooter and more than likely got himself in hot water. Todd had sentenced him to an open-ended vacation "anywhere out of California" until further notice.

Alpha males occasionally had difficulty relinquishing power to authority figures, and Zack was no exception. He absolutely, positively *hated* to be frustrated when it came to doing his job…almost as much as he hated taking vacations.

At the moment he was in his ninth hour of vacation and could hardly face the prospect of another minute, let alone an indefinite period of accomplishing absolutely nothing. The heavens had been raining on him since he'd left Los Angeles, doing a smear job on his recently detailed Lotus. To make matters worse, he also had a headache and a sore throat and feared he was coming down with a cold. He wasn't surprised. His good health seemed to be directly related to the skirmishes he fought in the war against crime. Constant challenge and sweet justice guaranteed high spirits and general well-being. No challenge whatsoever, not to mention a good dose of frustration, translated into sneezes and a cough. True to form, Zack began to pine for dry sheets and a box of tissues. When he sneezed his way into a one-stoplight town called Providence, he decided it was as good a place as any to spend the night.

It was dusk, and the rosy light slanting in from the west did wonderful things for the Lotus's platinum exterior finish. The exotic, hand-tooled car garnered him quite a bit of attention as he motored down good old "Main Street." None of his friends or colleagues would have recognized the low-slung sports car he drove, for the simple reason that he kept it hidden in his garage beneath a chamois car cover. Like the rest of the cops he knew, Zack drove a battered economy car with bad tires and too many miles. Anyone who planned on going into law enforcement for the money was doomed to great disappointment and poor transportation.

Though he looked, walked and talked like a cop, Zack had a few secrets he kept with religious fervor. Heaven help him if any of his buddies on the force found out that he had a genius IQ. Though his photographic memory was a tremendous help in his work, he played it down as much as he could. He couldn't help his intellectual gifts; he'd been born that way. Was it his fault that he had graduated summa cum laude from Berkeley with little effort and even less dedication? No. And so what if he happened to be a member of Mensa? Everyone had skeletons in their closets. Being labeled a genius had been seriously detrimental to his high school social life. He'd been saved from complete humiliation by securing the position of quarterback for the football team, guiding them to a state championship. All brains and no brawn would have made Zack a very dull boy.

At thirty-three, Zack was older and wiser, and by now an old hand at keeping his astonishing intellect under wraps. Still, certain challenges were irresistible to him. During his last year in college, he'd attended an economics lecture wherein the professor compared the chances of success in the stock market with the chances of success at a blackjack table in Vegas. Zack perked right up at the prospect of such an intriguing challenge. Immediately he had begun studying the stock market, quickly learning the ropes and spotting the trends. Initially he invested the small inheritance left to him by his father, and over the next few years created a fine bear market for himself. Simply put, he had become filthy rich. Not a soul on earth besides his banker and lawyer knew about his jaw-dropping fortune. Zack took great pains to keep it quiet, fearing his colleagues would no longer consider him "one of them" if they knew of his exalted tax bracket. Still, now and again he spoiled himself, as he had done when he'd impulsively purchased the Lotus. The only good thing about his vacation was the opportunity to bring his smoke-colored road rocket out of hiding. There was no denying it; alpha males liked to go fast.

As Zack reined in the growling Lotus at a stoplight, a sign in the lighted window of Appleton's General Store caught his eye: "Beat the bug! Save money on all supplies for cold-and-flu season!" He pulled into the parking lot, only too happy to call it a night. He was knee-deep in his own personal cold-and-flu season. He could see a motel down the road with an electric-blue vacancy sign. In thirty minutes he would be seriously medicated and off to dreamland. When he awoke, another eight hours of his vacation would be history.

He climbed out of the car, hearing his popping spine protest the length of time he had been sitting in one position. Walking through a curtain of rain, he shook the water off his head like a black Lab fresh from a swim. He wore threadbare jeans frayed white at the knees, a gray T-shirt and an ancient brown leather jacket broken in to the consistency of soft butter. Unless he was called on to testify in court, these were his "work clothes." It was a happy day when he had been promoted to the rank of detective four years earlier and given permission to shed his barely there marine haircut and ugly-as-sin patrolman's uniform. Life was sweet, indeed; he had a perpetual green light to chase bad guys and help maintain order in the Los Angeles, California, pack.

Until now. Zack's vacation instructions from Captain Todd were simple: "Forget work and read a book or something." As far as Zack was concerned, Todd was a sadist. Still, on the way out of town, he had stopped at a bookstore and picked up a copy of *Stephen Hawking's Universe,* a book he would never have bought had he been hanging out with his buddies. Maybe a little light reading would help him pass the time.

The notice on the sliding-glass door told Zack he had only two minutes to find his cold supplies before the store closed. He took off at a slow jog, scanning aisles one through ten before he saw the medicines in aisle eleven. He collected an armful of fine and potent cold remedies, including cough syrup with a very high alcohol content. Meanwhile a young employee mopped the floor around Zack's sneakers, looking very irritated at the possibility that Zack would be responsible for his shift going thirty seconds overtime.

"Oh, chill out," Zack growled, sniffing. He was in no mood to be pestered by a pimply faced teenager. "Just tell me where the tissues are, kid."

"Right behind you," the clerk muttered, pointing with the handle of his mop. "Any closer and they would have bit you. Could you move it along? I can't mop the floor if you're standing on it."

Obviously, the kid didn't know who he was dealing with. Zack decided to be difficult, for no other reason than he was miserable and it seemed fair that everyone else in the world should be miserable, too. "I always have a hard time making a decision. On one hand, you've got the really soft, puffy kind, but there's also the kind with the lotion in it. Then you have to decide on one-ply or two-ply. And I pretty much prefer unscented, but that's sometimes hard to find. It's a dilemma, you know?"

"*There,* right in front of you. Second shelf from the top.

We've got puffy, we've got lotion, we've got scented and unscented. Okay?"

"I love small towns," Zack told the clerk with complete insincerity. "They're so personal. When I retire, I think I'll come right back here to good ol' Providence. Live out my golden years basking in the warmth of your old-fashioned hospitality."

"It's five past ten," the clerk pointed out, unimpressed with Zack's sarcasm. "We're officially closed. If you want your puffy tissues, you'd better get a move on before they close the registers."

Zack's headache was getting worse and he'd left his patience behind in California. "Well, you're not closing promptly at ten tonight, bud. You know why? Because I want to walk around and make sure I get everything I need. I'm coming down with something, you know. I want to be prepared."

The clerk glowered at him through his wire-rimmed glasses. "So tell me what you need and I'll help you find it…fast."

"That's the trouble, you know? You never know what you're forgetting till it's too late. I'll just mosey around and see what catches my eye. Maybe a hot-water bottle. Or maybe some herbal tea. And some vitamin C, my mom always said it was good for…my mom always said…*holy smoke!*"

Something—actually, someone—had caught his eye in a death grip. A woman breezed around the corner in a rush, obviously trying to beat the clock. She was tall, willowy, exotic-looking. Her waist-length hair whipped behind her in a multicolored curtain of honey-brown, ivory and dark gold. Her full-length black leather coat swung open, revealing a cream-colored sweater shot through with white sequins. Her jeans were black, her sexy, high-heeled leather boots a startling shade of cranberry red. Zack liked a woman who wore leather. Unfortunately, those very sexy boots were a poor choice for recently mopped linoleum.

Zack gleefully realized he was going to be called on to be heroic. He loved to be heroic. Everything happened at once. Her left boot started to skid. Her eyes met his, wide, startled and helpless. Those eyes were the clearest, brightest, most unusual shade of crystalline blue he had ever seen, fringed with outrageously long lashes. The light-diffused, shimmering color was a heart-stopping contrast to the rich summer tan gilding her flawless skin. Zack had to mentally slap himself to switch to hero mode, dropping his medical supplies and happily holding out his arms to catch the fragrant, feminine bundle that toppled into them.

She was a bit heavier than she looked, but he managed. For a wonderful moment he had her full weight, holding her high enough that her heels kicked above the slippery floor. He enjoyed it immensely.

"This is a really nice store," he commented, winking at the startled clerk. Suddenly the kid wasn't bothering him so much.

The young woman in his arms rolled her eyes, one of her heels connecting painfully with his shin. "Oh, dear," she said innocently when he winced. "I'm terribly sorry. If you don't mind, it would be best if you put me down before I accidentally kick you again."

"I do mind," Zack sighed. He could only hold her in the protective arms of the law for so long. "But I will put you down, because you asked politely and you're wearing very sharp heels. Feisty little thing, aren't you?"

Reluctantly he relinquished his hold. Her boots hit the ground walking. Just like that. He'd been dismissed.

"*What?*" Zack asked the back of her leather coat. "No thanks? No introduction? No love at first sight?"

She looked over her shoulder, fluttering her long lashes at him. He swore he could feel a breeze. "You're sort of cute, but I'm afraid you're a little cocky. Thanks for your help. Goodbye.''

"Shot down," the clerk said, watching her round the corner and disappear.

Zack sighed, nodding sadly. "In flames."

"I've never seen her in here before," the clerk went on in a slightly dazed tone, no longer quite so upset at working late. "I guess I would have remembered if I had. Boy, was she hot."

Zack stared him down with cool gray eyes, the same look he used on punk teenagers with an attitude. "Down, boy. Back to your mopping. Look here, someone has broken a bottle of cough syrup all over the floor. That's too bad."

"I'll never get out of here," the kid grumbled. "Hey, man, what's that on your shirt? You've got her watch or something caught on your button."

Zack looked down his nose at the middle of his chest. There was indeed a delicate silver chain dangling there; the clasp was caught in the loose thread from a button. "It's not a watch," he said, more to himself than the clerk. Carefully he untangled the almost weightless piece of jewelry from the front placket of his shirt. "It's a bracelet. Her initials are on the clasp…*H.S.* I wonder what they stand for."

"Heather," the clerk said promptly, his attention caught despite the heavy burden of working overtime. "She looks like a Heather to me. Hey, you want me to take her bracelet up front? I can have her paged."

"I can handle it." Zack, holding the beautiful bracelet up to the light, began to smile. He'd completely forgotten about his cold. His symptoms had magically disappeared. He'd also forgotten about his vacation. Suddenly he had a fine new challenge, and the anticipation gave him a second wind. He actually laughed out loud, then took off in pursuit.

Unfortunately, the sweet-smelling lady in leather had vanished. He checked each and every aisle, then jogged up to the front where a big-haired girl with white-frosted lips waited in front of a register. Zack had a killer smile. One of his former lady friends had once described it as a nuclear weapon. He used it now for all he was worth. "Hello, there. I know you're closing now, but I wondered if you could do me a little favor?"

She didn't even consider it. "It's past ten. My register is closed."

Zack stared at her, taken aback. Apparently the nuclear weapon had been a dud. This had never happened before. "Look, I need to talk to one of your customers. A young woman wearing a long, black leather coat. Have you seen her?"

The girl nodded, snapping her gum. "Yeah. She asked me where the rest rooms were."

"And you told her…?"

She opened her eyes wide. "*Duh.* I told her where they were."

Zack stopped being charming and reverted to cop mode. "Look, lady, the sooner you start cooperating, the sooner you can leave. Where are the damned…the rest rooms?"

Her colorless, Casper the Ghost lips pouted. "*Fine.* Go to the double swinging doors at the rear of the store. Take your first door to the left and go down the stairs. You'll see the signs. Hustle, will you? I've got a date tonight."

Poor guy, Zack thought, sketching her a mocking salute.

Truth be told, he was surprised at his own determination to track down a woman who clearly wasn't interested in being tracked down. He simply wasn't accustomed to being dismissed by an attractive woman. It wasn't so much that he was an egotist, he'd simply learned long ago to expect and receive special treatment from the ladies. He didn't know if it was the cop thing or what, but women usually found him kind of appealing. Most women, anyway.

He did have his pride to consider. He had no intention of following the lovely lady into the women's rest room. That would look too desperate, not to mention somewhat indecent. Still, there was no law about waiting for her in the vicinity. After all, he was a Good Samaritan trying to do her a favor. His motives were almost selfless.

Smiling to himself, he followed the cashier's directions, going to the back offices of the store and through the double doors marked with an Employees Only notice, then opening the stairwell door. It was a heavy fire door, made of dull gray steel and posted with a No Exit sign. Another sign below this read, Authorized Personnel Only. Below that, Shoplifters Will Be Prosecuted to the Full Extent of the Law. Zack decided this was the least friendly store he had ever patronized.

Other than a single yellow lightbulb swinging from the ceiling, the hallway was in shadows. His face split with a grin, Zack squatted and looked at the sliver of light beneath the door of the women's rest room. He wasn't a detective for nothing, no sir. Now all he had to do was hurry up the stairs, station himself by the door of many signs and gallantly return her bracelet. She would have no choice but to introduce herself. He didn't know why it was so important that he know her name, but it was. His extraordinary intellect, combined with years of detective work, had left him with amazing powers of observation and recall. She had been wearing large, glittering earrings, obviously paste, but still nice. On close inspection her black coat was not leather at all, but a less-expensive imitation. Besides the thin silver chain around her wrist, she'd also worn a chunky men's digital watch, an inexpensive Timex if he wasn't mistaken. Most important, she had not been wearing a wedding ring. If he remembered accurately, she'd had a ring on every finger, with the single exception of her ring finger. It was a very important finger.

He heard the doorknob to the women's room rattle a bit, and quickly loped up the stairs three at a time. He didn't want to scare her by waiting in the hallway like some stalker. He'd go back into the well-lit storeroom and...and...

He tried the fire door a second time, with more force.

It was locked.

He winced as he heard her come out into the hallway. He was caught like a rabbit in a snare. This was going to severely affect his dignity. He remained rooted to the spot, hot blood burning his cheeks as he listened to the click, click, click of her heels moving down the hallway.

"Excuse me?" said a curious voice from the bottom of the stairs. "What are you doing up there?"

Zack's forehead thumped loudly against the steel door. "Me? Oh, I'm just being perplexed."

"Perplexed? Is there a problem? I know you're closing soon. I'm sorry if I delayed you."

Clearly she had mistaken him for someone who worked there. He wished he did; it would have made his explanation so much easier. He took a deep breath and slowly turned around, grateful the shadows hid the telltale wildfire in his face. "Hello, there. Fancy seeing you here."

"You?" she asked, her eyebrows narrowing suspiciously. "What is this? Are you following me or what?"

"You should have your ego looked at. I think it's swollen." Zack had learned long ago to improvise with the best of them. It was one of his survival tools when working undercover. Feigning injured innocence, he pulled her bracelet from his pocket, swinging it from his fingers like a pendulum. "You left this tangled up with one of my buttons when you fell into my arms. I was simply trying to return it to you. Sorry, but no ulterior motives. You're sort of cute, but you're a little cocky."

Now it was her turn to blush. "Oh. I suppose I jumped to the wrong conclusion."

"Like a kangaroo." Biting back a smile, Zack tossed her the bracelet, and she caught it in midair with a neat flick of her wrist. "Nice catch," he murmured appreciatively. He loved a woman with good hand-eye coordination.

"Thank you," she muttered, fastening the bracelet on her wrist. "This bracelet has tremendous sentimental value to me. I don't know what I would have done if I'd lost it."

"No problem." Unfortunately, the words reminded Zack there was, in fact, a major problem. Once again he tried to open the door. He tried it again. Finally he slammed his hip against the stubborn metal. "*Ouch.* That'll leave a mark. Listen, I hate to tell you this, but it seems we're locked in."

"*What?*" an alarmed voice directly behind him asked. "Locked in? As in *locked in?* We can't get out?"

Zack jumped, unaware that she had come up the stairs. He looked over his shoulder, feeling the jolt of her stabbing blue eyes a mere twelve inches from his. Even in the shadows, they seemed an intensely brilliant source of light. Her skin was golden, her generous lips stained wetly with a rich cinnamon gloss. This was the sort of woman who could give a sought-after ladies' man a run for his money...so to speak.

"We can't get out," Zack confirmed hoarsely, trying not to stare at that full-bloom rosebud mouth. "Not till they come and find us, at any rate."

"Are you kidding me? Tell me you're kidding me." Then, a full octave higher, "We're trapped?"

"Think positively," Zack encouraged. "We're not so much trapped as we are very, very secure."

"I'm *claustrophobic!*" she yelped, losing her cool. She pushed past him, jerking on the handle with both hands and nearly knocking Zack off the steps in the process. "I can't deal with this, I tell you. I have to know I can get out of places I go into. If I feel trapped, sometimes I...sometimes I panic and..."

"And what?" Zack asked warily, looking at her dilated pupils. "Oh-oh. You don't look so good. Sometimes you *what?*"

"I...do...this," she muttered weakly. And for the second time in less than ten minutes, she collapsed into Zack's waiting arms.

TWO

Anna Smith had never been the kind of person who came unglued easily, and never in public in front of a stranger. She had a little stubborn streak. Which was why, even as the little stairwell in Appleton's General Store was spinning into nauseating darkness, she was absolutely exasperated with herself. This was so *pathetic* for a twenty-six-year-old woman.

Fortunately, she wasn't completely out of it. She managed to more or less walk on her Gumby legs, supported by two strong arms and a bright, bracing stream of encouragement: "You can do it, here we go, down the stairs...good girl, good girl..."

He had a nice voice, she thought groggily. And very calm, almost like he was used to dealing with emergencies like this all the time. He dragged her along, finding an unlocked door close to the stairs. He turned on the light, and Anna found herself firmly planted in a hard folding chair.

"You okay?" he asked sharply, clicking his fingers in

front of her fluttering, half-closed eyes. "Hello, there! Yoo-hoo! Coming around? You can open your eyes, we've got a nice big room here. No windows, but...we won't think about that. You've got a door you can walk in *and* out of. Isn't that nice? We still can't get out of the basement, but...we won't think about that, either. If you don't say something soon, I'm going to use up all the oxygen blabbering." A pause, then in a more hopeful tone, "I suppose I *could* try artificial respiration."

"Don't you dare," Anna muttered, trying to control her weighty lids. "You know perfectly well that I'm breathing. Of all the idiotic things for me to do, fainting like that..."

Zack watched sympathetically while she tried to bury her swimming head in her knees. He'd been in a similar position himself many times after a rowdy night on the town. "That's it, take slow, deep breaths. You'll feel better soon." Then, with humor, "If it makes you feel better, I have this effect on women all the time. They're swooning here, there and everywhere."

Slowly, her white-knuckled hands clutching the seat of the chair, Anna forced herself to sit up straight. She saw they were in a very large storeroom of sorts, which caused her to breathe a great sigh of relief. As long as she didn't think about the locked door at the top of the stairs, she should be able to keep the demon claustrophobia at bay. "This is so embarrassing. I suppose I should thank you for catching me."

"Not if it's painful for you," Zack replied, hearing the reluctance in her voice. "Something tells me you're one of those women who don't need assistance too often."

She gave him a wobbly smile, her eyes still a bit glazed. "And something tells me you're used to women who very much appreciate your assistance. I'm doing better now. This chair feels like it's bobbing on the ocean, but other than that, I'm fine. This kind of thing doesn't happen all the time, just so you know."

"Freaking out was understandable in these circumstances," Zack replied. "We're all human, you know. Except Captain Todd, the bane of my existence. He's another species altogether."

She blinked in slow motion, her brows drawn together. "What are you talking about? Who is Captain Todd?"

Zack grinned, shaking his head. "Never mind. Since you're lucky enough not to know him, we'll keep it that way."

There was a long silence while Anna absorbed the full effect of his remarkable smile. She was clearheaded enough to translate the potent, wickedly sensual message he was delivering. His heavy-lidded gray eyes went along for the ride, as well, curling up at the edges in captivating little sunbursts. She saw sweetness there, and a silky-smooth masculine appeal that no doubt went over very well with the ladies. His thick hair was dark as midnight, a bit damp and carelessly finger-combed back from his face. He wasn't exceptionally tall, just under six feet, but he had the build of a lean young athlete. Even his well-worn leather jacket couldn't disguise the hard stretch of well-defined chest muscles beneath the soft gray T-shirt he wore. Anna found her eyes skipping lower, to the low-riding, stonewashed jeans that were more white than blue. She couldn't help it; he was standing and she was sitting, and the flat plane of his stomach and hips was directly at eye level. Altogether a dazzling and heady package…and here she was without sunscreen or shades. She couldn't help but shake her head at the voyeuristic trend of her thinking.

"*Ahem.*" Zack cleared his throat, more than a little self-conscious. She was studying him in precisely the same way he usually studied an attractive woman. Not in a rude way, but unusually candid. In his experience, and he had quite a bit of it, women tended to be a little flustered around him. He liked being the one who did the flustering, not the one *being* flustered. Having the tables turned wasn't nearly as much fun. "You're suddenly very quiet. Are you sure you're feeling all right?"

"I'm fine." Anna stood up slowly, telling herself to get a grip. "Excuse me. I was distracted by…never mind what I was distracted by."

"If you told me your name," Zack ventured, "I could scratch our initials in the fire door out there to commemorate our incarceration."

She smiled at that. "I'm Anna Smith, occasional fainter. We're in a little predicament here, I guess."

You guess right, Zack thought with gentle humor. *Lucky us.* "Nice to meet you. I'm Zack Daniels, catcher of fainting women. You make a very stimulating predicament partner, do you know that? And I'm an expert at predicaments *and* partners, so I speak with authority."

Anna decided he was harmless enough, despite his inclination to flirt. And he did provide nice scenery for their predicament. "Well, here's hoping we won't be partners for long. No offense, but this place isn't my idea of a dream vacation. Hey!"

Alarmed, Zack jumped and looked over his shoulder. "What? Who? Hey *what?*"

"I see a telephone!" She made her way through a pile of boxes, lifting up a bright pink telephone from beneath a sheet of clear plastic bubble wrap. "Of course, they would have a phone down here. Why didn't we think…" Her voice trailed off. She lifted her head, sheepishly meeting Zack's dancing eyes. "It's a Barbie phone."

Zack nodded, not even trying to hide his grin. This just kept getting better and better. She was a laugh a minute. "The Barbie sticker kind of gives it away, don't you think?"

"I can't believe my luck tonight…or absence thereof." She dropped the phone back in the box with a heavy sigh. "Oh, my goodness. Why can't anything be easy? Do you think there might be a phone in one of the other rooms?

Maybe there's another exit somewhere, or maybe a base-ment window we can crawl out of.''

"I doubt it. The sign on the fire door said No Exit.'' Zack was enjoying himself immensely. She was pure magic to watch, the way her changing emotions were reflected in her vivid eyes, her lips, the light catching the burnished-gold streaks in her hair whenever she moved. Nothing was hid-den, nothing was calculated. He couldn't remember the last time he'd met a woman who didn't try to impress him. They liked his looks, which he guessed was understandable. Not so understandable was their starry-eyed fascination with the potential danger involved with his work. The possibility of Zack being on the receiving end of severe bodily harm was inexplicably titillating to them. It wasn't very nice of them, but then again, Zack had never really focused on *nice* women. "I'm sure they'll find us sooner or later. Why don't you relax?''

She wrinkled her nose at him. "You've got to be kidding. I'm not the type who sits around expecting to be rescued. I'm perfectly capable of rescuing myself.''

"An independent and resourceful woman,'' Zack said re-spectfully, settling himself in the folding chair she had va-cated. "How inspiring. I'll sit here and admire your re-sourceful character while you rescue us. You may begin.''

Obviously, he wasn't taking this situation of theirs very seriously. Ignoring him, Anna proceeded to explore the room at length, rummaging through piles of boxes, cleaning supplies and office equipment...but no telephone. She went to the door twice, giving the darkened hallway a quick look before scuttling back into the room. "You could do some-thing,'' she told Zack irritably, annoyed by his complacent attitude and Cheshire Cat smile. "I'm not keen on exploring the other rooms. I feel trapped whenever I look out there. Would it be too much bother for you to separate yourself from that chair and look around?''

"Well, I suppose I could take a look around,'' Zack said

after a moment of reflection. He stood up and slowly stretched, his sparkling eyes noting her reaction with amusement. "I do have a little cold and I'm feeling under the weather, but I'll manage somehow. Still, I hate to leave you in here all alone, you being so delicate and all. Will you be all right without me?"

Anna placed a hand over her heart with exaggerated sincerity. "I will do my poor best."

Zack grinned. "Lady, you're the most entertaining thing that has happened to me in my entire life. I'll be right back. Don't move a muscle."

He was gone for several minutes. Anna heard doors opening and closing, boxes being shoved around and occasional sounds of exaggerated discouragement. Then she heard him knocking on the fire door and calling out for someone to help them, all to no avail. When he came back, he had an expression of utter dejection, though his keen gray eyes were still lit with enjoyment. "We are doomed, my pretty new predicament partner. No exits, no windows, no way to call anyone. And there's not a sound from upstairs. I'm afraid they may have locked things up and left. I can't tell you how upset I am about this. We have ourselves in a pickle here. Or rather, a pickle jar with a very tight lid."

"Well, this is just wonderful," Anna muttered, hands planted on her hips over her leather coat. "Absolutely *wonderful*. What on earth do we do now? I'm not about to spend an entire night locked in some basement, I'll tell you that."

"I'm afraid," Zack said kindly, "you are."

She stared at him suspiciously. "You know something? I think you *like* this situation."

Zack could have told her he was tickled hot pink with the whole thing, but he didn't think the timing was right. He settled with, "Let's just be happy it isn't Saturday night. If it was and the store wasn't open on Sundays, we could be here all weekend. We wouldn't have any food except for gummy bears and candy necklaces, and—"

"What's that?" Anna was instantly distracted from their little problem. Zack Daniels had just mentioned her favorite food group: candy. Besides, it just wasn't in her nature to be grumpy for too long. "You really found gummy bears?"

Grinning like a proud hunter, home with his kill, Zack pulled a cellophane bag from his jacket pocket, swinging it from his fingers in front of Anna's nose. "I found a whole case of gummy bears and two cases of candy necklaces. Oh, yes—and games. Candyland, Monopoly, Twister. We can find all kinds of things to keep us occupied." He slowly uncoiled his teasing, bone-melting smile again, making the room seem suddenly smaller and a great deal warmer. "Trust me, Anna Smith. I'm an expert when it comes to handling predicaments."

"And now we'll have sharing time," Zack announced in his best Sunday school teacher's voice.

Anna's baby blues narrowed. She was nobody's fool; she had nixed the idea of playing Twister right off the bat. Instead, they had spent an hour playing the ever-popular board game, Candyland. Despite Zack's dark mutterings about "sissy games," he played along like a good sport and emerged the winner. After that they'd found a chess game. Again Zack won. He never seemed to need any time at all to ponder his next move, yet his strategy was astonishing. The win, he claimed, meant that it was now his turn to choose the next activity.

"And what precisely do you want to *share* during sharing time?" Anna asked cautiously. She was leaning with her back against the wall, legs stretched out before her. Her boots were off, as was her long black coat. Zack sat opposite, leaning against a four-foot-high box of paper towels with his jacket for a pillow, chewing on a candy necklace he was wearing.

"*Stuff.*" He grinned, wriggling his eyebrows like the evil villain Snidely Whiplash. He'd been flirting shamelessly throughout the chess game, inspired by the way she slowly ran her tongue along the edge of her upper lip when pondering her next move. Unfortunately, he hadn't seen much progress. Anna took every teasing comment he made in stride, easily holding her own. She was accustomed to men flirting with her. She didn't think it was so much her looks that were inspiring the attention as much as it was the basic nature of men. It had become tiresome, to say the least. While in high school, she had first heard the old saying, "Men never make passes at girls who wear glasses." She had gone right out and purchased a pair of non-prescription eyeglasses, but the old adage had proved false. Glasses or no glasses, she was destined to be the target of masculine interest. She realized early on that very few of her admirers were interested in her fine character, lively sense of humor or steadfast loyalty. Nine times out of ten, it was a purely physical attraction, something along the lines of, "Lie down, I think I love you."

Anna had learned to cope quite well, and wasn't thrown a bit by Zack's obvious interest. When he complimented her on her glorious, waist-length hair, she told him his own razor-cut style was very flattering for his square-jawed face. Appalled, he immediately went on the defensive. He did *not* have his hair styled, he had it *cut,* plain and simple. Anna had opened her big blue eyes very wide and innocently apologized. It seemed to her that the man wasn't used to being frustrated by women.

"Whatever." She shrugged. "At least this is one game you can't actually beat me at. I'm a kindergarten teacher, so I'm very experienced when it comes to sharing time."

"I never, *ever* had a kindergarten teacher who looked like you. If I had, I would have put off going into first grade for a few years. So, anyway, we'll take turns asking each other questions. If we choose *not* to answer, we have to take a dare."

"That's not the way we have sharing time in kindergarten."

"Of course it isn't. We're adults, darn it, and we'll have sharing time like adults."

"Says the man who is wearing a candy necklace. Okay, you won Candyland and the chess game, so I get to go first. Yes?"

"Well..." Zack nodded, somewhat suspicious. "I guess so."

Anna tipped her head back against the wall, popping another couple of gummy bears into her mouth. "Okay. When was the last time you cried?"

"What?" Zack immediately gagged on his candy. This was completely unacceptable. Despite the fact he was wearing a necklace, he was a macho kind of guy through and through. He usually carried a *gun,* for Pete's sake. Men who wore guns did not admit to crying. He couldn't think of a single male friend who would even admit to having tear ducts. "You've got to be kidding me, right?"

"Wrong. I'm serious."

"That's ridiculous! No way am I answering that." If he did, he would have to tell her he shed a couple of tears a week earlier when he saw *Where The Red Fern Grows* on late-night television. "Ask me something else. Anything."

She shrugged, cheerfully biting the head off a gummy bear. "No way. You can't pick and choose your questions."

"Oh, but I can." He took off his candy necklace for emphasis, throwing it over his shoulder. "I don't care what you ask me, it can't be as bad as the first question."

"You don't think so?" She tilted her head sideways, studying him with mischief in her electric-blue eyes. For the first time since leaving Grayland Beach, she was actually having a good time. Zack Daniels was more than just a pretty face—or rather, good-looking face. He was funny, incredibly quick-witted and an entertaining verbal sparring partner. Anna had never made the mistake of thinking good looks were an indication of a good nature, but she did appreciate the diversion. What woman wouldn't? "I'm going to enjoy this," she said, rubbing her hands together with great anticipation. "Okay, I'll take pity on you and ask you another question. When was the last time you lied?"

Zack winced. Actually, the last time he'd lied had been about two hours earlier, when he'd told her how upset he was that they were locked in the basement. "Having sharing time was a bad idea. I've changed my mind. I don't want to play anymore."

"Don't be such a chicken."

"I'm not a chicken, I'm a dignified male who refuses to look stupid." He paused, giving her an "I dare you to make me" look. "Keep this up and I'm going to start chipping away at the concrete wall with my pocketknife to escape from here. You're a threat to my masculinity, do you know that? And I've only known you for—" he consulted his watch "—one hour and fifty-five minutes. You're scary."

Anna laughed, throwing back her head and slapping her palms on her jeans-clad thighs. "And you're easy. Round one goes to me. Finally I win at something."

Zack opened his mouth to deliver a delightfully witty comeback, then promptly forgot the words. She made a heart-stopping picture, this vibrant, light-filled creature with soul-piercing eyes and clouds of bright hair swirling around her shoulders. Her sweater was tight enough to show she was a woman and loose enough to show she was a lady. His eyes slid over the entire fetching picture, lingering on her shoeless feet. Here was another surprise. Her black stockings were shot through with glittering silver question marks. And her toes curled when she laughed. She was an original.

He sighed heavily, for the moment giving up on being witty. He was certainly man enough to show he wasn't immune to her extraordinary charm. Besides, he wanted to further distract her from sharing time. "I have to tell you

something," he said, tilting his head sideways in a panto-
mime of thoughtful consideration. "You are definitely the
most beautiful woman I have ever seen in my entire life."

She lifted her eyebrows curiously, as if waiting for him
to make his point.

"That was a *compliment*," Zack explained, in the tone
of one speaking to the mentally impaired. Never had he
experienced so much trouble trying to get into a little trouble. "What is it with you? You never react to anything quite
the way I expect."

She shrugged, finishing off the last surviving gummy
bears. "Who says how someone should react to things? I
have this friend named Frank, and he has the most amazing
analytical mind. He always tells me the world would be a
much saner place if people *acted* and not *reacted*. It makes
sense, don't you think?"

"Frank?" Zack said, reacting for all he was worth. "Who
is Frank?"

"I told you, he's my friend. He's a judge, so you can
imagine how interesting he is. When he sits on the bench,
he looks just like an avenging angel, with his black robe
and silver hair."

"Silver hair?" Zack seized on that one immediately.
"Then he's old?"

Anna frowned at him. "No, he just has prematurely silver
hair. It's beautiful. As I was saying, Frank contends that
emotions are something to be governed, not something that
governs us. He talks like that, kind of stuffy. But he's fascinating to listen to, and the stories he tells—"

"I don't like Frank," Zack told her, sounding a little
stuffy himself. "I don't want to talk about Frank. If I had
a really ugly dog, I would name him Frank."

"You don't even know Frank. I swear, you're just like
Davy."

"Oh, hell." Zack stood up, mentally adding frustrating

to the list of words that described this surprising woman. "And Davy would be…?

"Davy is also a friend. He's what you would call a man's man, someone who lives for hunting season and fishing season and any other manly season you can think of. He also likes to climb very high mountains. My point is, like you, he has a tendency to—"

"Don't you have any friends who are women?"

"Not many, actually. My father was a high school football coach. The players were always coming to the house. I met some of my best friends that way. Anyway, when Davy isn't off hunting elk or climbing mountains, he takes his shirt off and models for covers of romance novels. You might have seen his picture."

The light of battle flared in Zack's eyes. "Are you suggesting I read romance novels?"

"No, although I don't know why that would bother you. The point I am *trying* to make—"

"Wait a minute," said Zack. "Do I *look* like a model to you?"

"This is ridiculous. Will you put a lid on your testosterone and listen? Like many macho men, Davy is someone who has been known to react emotionally rather than think things through."

A tiny muscle went tic-tic-tic in Zack's hard brown cheek. "Well, I am *not* someone who reacts emotionally. I am in complete control of myself at any given moment. Cool, calm and collected. Ask my buddies how well I discipline my emotions if you don't believe me."

"I see," she said in a sweet voice. "You never do anything impulsively."

"I'm saying that I have incredible self-control." Reflecting on this, Zack realized that anyone who knew him well would be rolling on the floor and laughing hysterically about now. Especially Captain Todd. "How did we get on this subject, anyway? Considering we just met, don't you think you're making way too many assumptions about me?''

"I'm sorry. I do that, draw conclusions about people right off the bat. I don't really judge them, I just look in their eyes and…sort of feel what they're all about. It's a gift I have.'' Humming beneath her breath, Anna picked her way through boxes, files and crates, searching for something more nutritious than candy. "People usually give off vibes, and I really do believe you can look into someone's eyes and read them.''

Zack followed her zigzag pattern across the room, bound and determined to make his point. "I want you to understand something. In my line of work, I can't afford to be affected by personal emotions. I'm told that I'm very good at what I do, so obviously I have the ability to remain calm and focused on my objective. Also, unlike your friend Delbert—''

"Davy."

"Whatever. Unlike what's-his-bucket, I don't make a habit of living on an emotional seesaw. Besides, there is no way in the world you can look into someone else's eyes and know what they're like, what they're thinking or feeling. People have too many protective layers these days. It's a defense mechanism we all have. And considering the criminal elements in our society, it's a good thing to be cautious.''

"No one can keep their true nature hidden completely.''

"Ah, that's where you're wrong,'' Zack told her with the sage voice of experience. "I've known several people who could hide their true natures completely. Unless they choose to take the mask off, no one has a clue who they are or what they're capable of.''

"You seem awfully familiar with the 'criminal element.' You're not a criminal, are you?''

"Of course I'm not a criminal. Do I look like someone who could rob a bank?''

"Yes," Anna said instantly, grinning at the insulted look on his face. "And you also look like a person who wouldn't get caught, either. You're very...confident." She bent over, huffing and puffing as she struggled to lift one box off the other. "Look at the label on the box beneath this—beef jerky. Yippee! What *is* your line of work, anyway? No, wait. Let me guess. You look like you would be very photogenic. Are you a model?"

For the second time that night, but with even more fire, "The hell you say! Look, you're going to hurt yourself. Let me."

Anna was more than happy to move aside and let the big strong man lift the heavy box. "Okay, okay. I was just teasing. I'll be serious now. Let's see. There are any number of professions a man like you could be suited for. You're obviously familiar with a shady side of society. Are you a public defender?"

"Sort of," Zack replied. "I defend the public quite a bit, as a matter of fact. No more guesses? Use your ESP, Anna." He set the box on the floor and turned to her, both hands planted on his hips. "Can't you look in my eyes and know all my secrets?"

Anna's smile grew wider. "Oh, I've had you pegged from 'Hello.' Not your profession, maybe, but definitely your nature. You're a typical male—you like to win every game you play. You're so intelligent it's scary, you flirt like a pro and you've had enough experience with the world to make you a little cynical. You can also laugh at yourself, and you enjoy helping people. How am I doing so far?"

"Pretty good. Except that bit about me being typical." Zack teasingly fluttered his lashes at her. "I like to think I'm somewhat out of the ordinary."

She opened her eyes wide, speaking in a spooky, Vincent Price voice. "I can see into your soul, Zack Daniels. I know who you are inside and out."

Softly he said, "Lady, you haven't even scratched the

surface yet." Zack took one step, just enough to bring his sneakers and her stocking toes together. His eyes locked on hers, and his smile took on a slick and dangerous curve. This flirtatious, provocative dance was familiar ground for him. He was face-to-face with an incredibly appealing woman, and he was tired of being on the defensive. In addition to chess, there were certain other games he played very well; he had it on the best of authority. And he was getting increasingly hungry to play them with Anna. "I'm going to give you a chance to prove your point. Look in my eyes." He lowered his voice, imitating Anna's eerie delivery. "Tell me what I'm thinking, oh great and wonderful wizard. *Read* me."

Here was something new. The atmosphere between them changed in a heartbeat. One moment they were lighthearted and teasing, the next moment a sharp awareness slipped into the narrow space dividing their bodies, stealing their smiles in a sneak attack. Zack was suffocatingly close, seeming larger than life, every powerful physical attribute he possessed magnified ten times over. Anna stared mutely at the way his ragged lashes cast half-moon shadows on his cheeks, the sharp flecks of blue in his smoky gray eyes. She could smell the faintest hint of his cologne, something musky and very male. His glossy, jet-black hair was shimmering almost wetly beneath the overhead lights, a devilishly dark halo. She could feel him reaching out to her, urging, pulling at her. And she couldn't pretend not to understand the look in his restless gray eyes.

Her body was buzzing and tickling, her respiration coming in short, quick catches. She couldn't step back; she couldn't pull her eyes from his. Her lips parted on a strand of breath, her eyes widened with awareness.

Anna wasn't a woman who carelessly took risks, but suddenly she realized she *wanted* to walk the knife-edge line between safety and danger. Zack was virtually a stranger, which added a tantalizing dose of the unknown to the moment. He was charismatic, he was ultraconfident, he was one hundred percent male. And even if she wanted to, she couldn't get away from him until they were rescued. Zack Daniels and his hedonist's smile was temptation in the finest masculine incarnation she had ever seen.

As she studied his face, she deliberately allowed her imagination to wander into an unfamiliar and reckless curiosity. In an oddly distant way she knew she was safe. A brief lowering of her defenses wouldn't change that. In a matter of hours they would be going their separate ways, back to their own lives. She would never see him again. And meanwhile the chemistry sizzling between them was pressing her to experiment. Just a little, and no one but Anna and Zack would ever know. One short moment in time when consequences wouldn't matter.

Why not?

Three

"This is so strange," Anna said softly, her voice unnaturally husky. "When I stop and think—"

"The sad end to all waking dreams—*thinking*. Why do we have to stop and think? Haven't you ever wanted to do anything risky?" Even as he spoke, Zack's pulse continued to accelerate. He wondered if she had any idea of the beguiling, bewitching picture she made. Her small face was draped with gold and honey-colored hair that curled in looping question marks over her shoulders. *So sweet.*

Her beautiful eyes remained solemn. "Are you telling me you're risky?"

"Some people think so." His body moved infinitesimally closer to hers, drawn by something he couldn't see or explain. She was a hypnotizing contradiction of darkness and light, uncertainty and daring. With all his experience, Zack felt like a newborn, amazed that a situation that had begun so innocently could feel so sharply, aggressively sexual.

Thoughtfully she tilted her head to one side, unable to

stem her curiosity about this man. "Should I be careful, then?"

"No. Please, no." His hand slipped beneath her hair, warm on the delicate nape of her neck. Even as he lowered his face to hers, he was aware of an uncharacteristic trembling in his body. He saw her eyes grow wider, brighter, the dark rings of her irises visibly expanding. Then her face blurred, his attention fiercely riveted on her parted lips. The first tentative touch of his mouth on hers was the merest caress, a fluttering, barely there butterfly kiss. Still, the resulting shiver that coursed through his body was hard and unexpected. He heard the sharp intake of her breath, and a stark urgency flared to life within him. Whatever was happening here was happening to them both.

And he wanted more.

The second kiss went much deeper and demanded far more than the featherlight touch of butterfly wings. Zack slanted his head to capture her lips fully, his palms framing her face while he drank with a hunger that startled even him. At the same time Anna's hands closed over fistfuls of his T-shirt, clinging for dear life. She could feel steel in his muscles.

The fact that Zack was a virtual stranger sharpened the fiery sensations sparkling through her like champagne bubbles. And the way he made magic with his warm lips and cool tongue added the most delicious, sinfully wicked pleasure. She felt a curling heat deep in her stomach, a connection to this man and this moment that somehow went beyond a simple kiss. In an instant she somehow knew she had changed, never to be quite the same again.

When Anna finally pulled back from the kiss, she was feeling light-headed and weak all over. Her eyes had an endless depth as she studied his expression, hot and hectic with emotion. Like a dreamer she raised her hand to smooth back his hair, the silky strands flowing like cool water through her fingers. So soft, like she was playing with clouds. Her body had transformed into warm butter, barely holding its shape. One more second in his arms and she would have been pooled around his feet on the floor.

"I wonder why I did that," she said hoarsely.

"I know why I did," Zack replied, sounding a bit hoarse himself. "Do you have any idea what you do to a man? What just *looking* at you does to me?"

At that, she shook her head and smiled faintly. Obviously her own incredible looks didn't figure whatsoever in her value system. "You don't need to flatter me. For the moment there's no competition."

"I wasn't trying to—"

And then the real world tapped them on the shoulder.

From out in the hallway a door slammed, followed by a loud commotion of male voices. Zack said a four-letter word, then closed his eyes and took a heavy, sustaining breath. It was hard to go from sensual to sensible in the space of three seconds.

"We are about to be rescued," he growled, his eyes still closed tight. "And in my opinion the timing really sucks."

Anna was both relieved and disappointed. This was her safety hatch, her opportunity to run from this beguiling stranger before things got out of control. This was why she had allowed herself to be carried away, knowing that nothing about this night was real. She tried to smile, but she was overwhelmed by the confusing emotions shuddering through her. She dropped her hands awkwardly to her sides and stepped away from him. The air between them felt instantly cool, the fluorescent lights harsher and the atmosphere thick and uncomfortable. "I guess we should be grateful for the interruption. We're a very bad influence on each other."

The voices grew louder. Zack's eyes flew from Anna to the door and back to Anna again. "The last thing I am is grateful. Look, this whole thing wasn't—"

The door flew open, framing two uniformed policemen

and an amazingly short, triple-chinned man who had "Owner of Appleton's General Store" stamped all over him. Before either policeman had time to speak, he marched into the storeroom, obviously emboldened by his gun-toting companions. "*Ha!* I knew something fishy was going on the moment I spotted the car and the Jeep parked out front. What the devil do you think you're doing, breaking into my store?"

Zack scowled at him, feeling an overwhelming urge to pop the blowhard in the nose. However, since he was an officer of the law, he shoved his hands in his pockets and contented himself with speaking his mind. "I don't like you."

The man turned red, puffing out his barrel chest. "*What? * As a criminal, you are in no position to like or dislike anyone. In case you haven't noticed, you and your partner in crime have been apprehended."

Zack wasn't impressed. "Oh, put a cork in it. We're trying to break *out* of your store, buddy, not into it. We made the mistake of visiting the bathrooms around closing time and got locked in. You should have a sign posted at that door at the top of the stairs: Run Like Hell if the Clock Strikes Ten."

Looking acutely uncomfortable, one of the policemen politely cleared his throat. "Like I told you upstairs, Dad, I think you might be overreacting."

"Dad?" Zack asked incredulously. "This guy is your father?"

The young man nodded almost shamefacedly. "I'm afraid so. I mean, yes."

"Afraid?" the owner spouted, turning his indignant gaze on his son. "*Afraid?* Are you trying to say you're not proud to call me father? Is that what you're trying to say?"

The second policeman raised a calming hand. "Now, let's all cool down. Nothing has been disturbed upstairs, and these people would hardly leave their getaway vehicles in

full view in the parking lot for any passerby to see. I'm sure
this is nothing more than an unfortunate accident, Dad.''

"Dad?" Zack blurted again, his eyes growing wider by
the second. ''Good Lord, is everyone in this town an Appleton? If we *were* criminals, we'd be in big trouble here.
Talk about having the cards stacked against you.''

Anna's shoulders jumped with a half-born giggle, which
was quickly stifled by her hand. She couldn't help it; she
had a vivid imagination and this whole scene had the feel
of a Three Stooges movie. Curly and Moe were bumbling
policemen, and Larry was the befuddled villain.

''We don't get many criminal types through here, anyway,'' son number one replied with a regretful sigh. ''Being
a cop in Providence can be kind of boring, actually. Still,
hope on and hope ever, as our captain says. Are you both
all right?''

The older man again took offense. ''I don't believe you!
You're asking these trespassers if they're all right? You're
supposed to be the law around here, damn it! Why aren't
you arresting them? Do I have to slap the cuffs on them
myself?''

''They didn't do anything,'' son number two pointed out
in a long-suffering voice. ''And I told you before, I called
in the license plates on both cars. No problems. Besides,
this guy is a *cop,* Dad. Remember? They told me when I
ran the plates. I think you should take one of your nitro-
glycerin pills and go home.''

Anna looked at Zack. ''So that's what you do for a living.
You're a cop. That's perfect. It really does fit you much
better than being a lawyer.''

''There's something fishy going on here,'' Appleton Sr.
muttered. ''It's a trick, I tell you.''

''There are *way* too many policemen in this room,'' Zack
announced. Not only had a beautiful moment had been cut
short, but he was growing increasingly irritated with the

short guy's testosterone tantrum. "I think it's time for the lady and me to take our leave."

Anna gave the Appleton boys a dazzling smile. "Can we please leave now, Mr. Policemen?"

The officers bobbed their heads like two dashboard puppies, obviously pleased to grant this stunning lady's wish. Their outraged father sputtered and coughed, but both Zack and Anna ignored him. They collected their coats and took the stairs two at a time, leaving a family argument boiling over in the basement of Appleton's General Store.

Anna found herself avoiding Zack's eyes as he escorted her to her forest-green Jeep in the parking lot. Somehow, what had seemed so natural and enticing while locked in a basement now felt rather embarrassing. Apparently even a brief stolen moment could have consequences. "What a night," she said, anxious to fill the thick silence. Every second that ticked by seemed to increase her feeling of awkwardness. Kissing a stranger while they were locked up in a basement together was one thing. Facing him as they returned to reality was a bit sticky. "I thought we'd never get out of there."

"Will you slow down a little? This isn't the fifty-yard dash. Anna—"

"I can't believe it's nearly one in the morning. I didn't plan on my visit to the store to last half the night. All I wanted was some Tums." She unlocked her car, tossing him a tight little smile over her shoulder. "I've been under a little stress lately, and my stomach doesn't like stress. I remember once when—"

"Look, hang on a minute. You're talking faster than a trained parrot. What on earth is wrong with you?"

"Not a thing, not a single thing. I was just…just…" She was suddenly distracted by the car parked very near to hers. Obviously his car, since they were the only two in the parking lot. It was a Lotus, a sleek, silvery work of art. A terribly expensive work of art. This was the sort of car she found mention of in magazines like Fortune and Forbes. "That isn't…that isn't your car, is it? That thing has to cost more money than I'll make in my lifetime."

"Uh…maybe I'm a very good cop," Zack mumbled, momentarily caught off guard. Apparently his rapid-fire intellect was adversely affected by a pair of big blue eyes. It was a humbling moment.

Anna giggled nervously. "Policemen don't make that kind of salary, do they? Because if they do, I'm off to the police academy first thing tomorrow."

With a sinking heart, Zack saw a new expression on her face, a combination of confusion, curiosity and distance. This was the same expression he had feared he would one day see on his friends' faces should they ever discover he was such an oddity—a rich cop. Besides, how would he explain to Anna how he amassed his fortune? *Actually, I'm a genius. I played the stock market for a couple of months just for fun and ended up with several million dollars. Go figure.*

"I'm just teasing you," he said after an almost imperceptible pause. "It's not my car. You're right about cops' salaries, we barely make enough to pay for our donuts. The Lotus…an inheritance from my father. Can we talk about something extremely pertinent to this moment? Like where the devil you're going in such a rush?"

"You know…places to go, things to do when I get there. Well, it's been an unforgettable experience." She turned to face him, sticking out her hand. "Nice meeting you, Zack. You've been an entertaining companion."

Entertaining? Zack could have sworn that something more went on in that basement than simple entertainment. Again, a humbling moment. "What is this? Do you have a split personality or what? Unless I miss my guess, about ten minutes ago we were lip-locked and loving it."

Anna turned her back on him, fumbling for the Jeep's door handle. Her face felt as if it was on fire. If nothing else, she'd learned a little lesson about the awkward consequences of giving in to one's base desires. Sooner or later you had to face reality. "Sure. It was fun."

"Fun?" In the past being tagged as "fun" hadn't bothered Zack at all. Tonight, however, the innocent little word felt like a slap in the face. He reached out and took hold of Anna's shoulders, firmly turning her to face him. "I didn't notice you laughing hysterically. I *did* notice your breathing getting out of control and your hands trembling when I kissed you. Was that part fun, too?"

"Yes," Anna said stubbornly. "When my fingers are trembling, I know I'm having fun. Fun, fun, fun."

Zack wasn't amused. "Why do you need to run off like this?"

"I'm late."

"Late for what?"

"I'm late for arriving at the place where I'm going." Wherever that was. Anna deftly twisted free of his touch, opening the car door and climbing inside. She knew she was acting like a schizophrenic, but she couldn't seem to control herself tonight. As good old Frank would say, she was reacting instead of acting. "I'm a very punctual person."

"That's wonderful," Zack snapped childishly. "*Fine*. It's been real, kiddo."

Biting down hard on her lip, she looked up at him, her lavish blue eyes briefly giving away her confusion. She knew this was the point where she should start the car and drive away, but her fingers simply weren't cooperating. Strange. A couple of hours ago she had found comfort in the thought that he would soon disappear from her life. Now that knowledge was oddly depressing. "Well…"

Zack looked at the ground, scuffing the toe of his sneaker on the asphalt. "Don't let me keep you."

"I'll be seeing you."

At that his head snapped up, staring hard into her eyes.

"No, you won't. You don't even know where I live, and I don't know where you live. And obviously you're content to leave it that way."

Anna was silent for a long moment, though she never broke eye contact. "I think it's better this way," she said finally. "I'm not...I don't usually do this kind of thing. I'm a pretty humdrum kind of person."

"What kind of thing?" Zack demanded. "Kissing men? Are you a nun or something? Nuns don't usually wear black leather coats."

She smiled faintly. "Maybe I'm a trendsetting nun."

"You're really going," Zack said, more to himself than to her. He'd dated his last girlfriend for six months, but it hadn't really bothered him when they'd parted ways. After only a couple of hours, letting Anna Smith disappear from his life was surprisingly difficult. Besides, his pride was killing him. He didn't have much experience in *not* making an impression on a woman. "And I can't make you change your mind?"

"I can't afford to change my mind," Anna replied with a wistful smile. "I'm not very good at complications. I'm one of those weird people who like predictability. I have my life all organized and cozy, waiting to welcome me home. Nothing remarkable, but it suits me perfectly. Besides, tonight was..." Her voice trailed off. She looked down at her lap, drumming her fingers on the steering wheel.

"Tonight was...?" Zack prompted.

"Perfect just the way it was." She sighed, leaning her head back against the seat. "The rain has finally stopped. Can you smell how fresh the air is? I love it when the world is all fresh and clean like this."

Obviously the subject had been changed. Since he truly didn't know what else to do, Zack bent down, pressing his lips softly to her forehead. Then he stepped back, closing the Jeep's door. "So be it. At least I tried."

She gave him one last look, feeling the strange tug of unfamiliar emotions. Then, because she hadn't really left herself any choice, she started the car and pulled out of the parking lot.

Immediately Zack pulled a pen out of his pocket and wrote her license plate number on the palm of his hand. He wasn't through trying...not by a long shot.

Alpha males never gave up.

The motel Zack had seen earlier was managed by a middle-aged woman with a Santa Claus figure and a headful of pink foam curlers. She didn't like being roused from her sleep, judging by the expression on her face. Zack threw her a preoccupied smile, and she started to blush and fiddle with the rick-rack collar of her pink-and-white seersucker robe. Wonderful. *Now* the nuclear weapon worked. Immediately he whipped out his poker face and asked if he could pay half price for only using the room half the night. He had discovered long ago that businesswomen didn't mind being friendly—*unless* it cost them money. This lady was no exception: "A pretty face won't get you any special treatment here," she snapped, abandoning her flirtatious air.

Climbing the metal-grate stairs to his room on the second floor, Zack brooded on his unhappy existence, feeling deeply sorry for himself. A stout woman with curlers in her hair had just called him pretty. Before that, an irresistible woman had resisted him with no trouble at all. He'd kissed her and she'd kissed him back, which was probably a good thing, except for the fact that he now knew exactly what he was missing. Yes, he had Anna Smith's license plate number, but that didn't guarantee he'd ever see her again. The Jeep could be borrowed or rented for all he knew. He'd call in the license plate number first thing in the morning and discover just how depressed he should be. He knew that Anna wasn't going to be easy to track down. And why?

Because he was on vacation and bad things happened to people when they were on vacation.

Though Zack had supposedly been given a nonsmoking room, it smelled heavily of cigarette smoke. He had quit smoking five years earlier, a monumental achievement for a man who had been smoking since he was sixteen. But suddenly he was itching for a cigarette. Naturally he blamed his renewed cravings on his burdensome vacation. The dripping faucet in the bathroom, the air conditioner that refused to turn off and the mattress that seemed to be made out of cement he also blamed on his vacation. It was a fine scapegoat.

He stripped off his clothes and huddled beneath the lightweight bedspread trying to get warm. After a few minutes he put his clothes back on and dove beneath the covers, trying to block out the rumbling of the air-conditioning. He didn't feel sleepy whatsoever. Every time he closed his eyes, he saw Anna. She was grinning at him over her shoulder, fluttering her extravagant lashes and looking so damned adorable. *You're cute, but you're a little cocky.*

Why had he let her go? Why hadn't he *done* something?

It was rare for a woman to have this effect on Zack. Since his life was his work, he'd always made a practice of ending his relationships long before either party was seriously involved. He had learned from firsthand experience how difficult it was for someone in his line of work to have a normal private life. Zack's father had also been a cop, a larger-than-life hero to his son and a man respected among his colleagues for his courage, humor and loyalty.

Unfortunately, Tommy Daniels was far better at enforcing the law than he was at making his marriage to his wife, Kelly, a success. Whether it was due to his addiction to thrills and chills or his famous roving eye, Tommy was a bitter and recurring disappointment to the woman who waited at home for him. Zack's mother had tried for fifteen years to hold her marriage together. Though Tommy loved his wife, he was a man who became bored easily and found it difficult to enjoy the stifling responsibilities of a husband and father. He couldn't relate to his wife's loneliness, or her constant anxiety about his well-being. If *he* was content, why wasn't she? Toward the end of their unhappy marriage, Kelly had begged her husband to leave his job and concentrate on his family. For Tommy, that was like asking him to give up oxygen for the rest of his life.

Zack had been only thirteen years old when his parents finally divorced, but he was mature enough to realize the toll his father's career had taken on the woman who had made the mistake of loving him. It was hard for him to reconcile his larger-than-life hero with the same man who had hurt his mother so deeply and so easily.

After surviving nearly twenty years as a homicide detective, Tommy Daniels died from sunstroke during a deep-sea fishing trip in Cabo San Lucas. Such an ironic twist of fate for a man who had reveled in life, luck and chance. Kelly had subsequently married a tax accountant who had come home every night at 5:00 p.m. and never forgot her birthday or anniversary. With her new husband, Kelly found stability, security and appreciation. If she never looked at him quite the way she used to look at her first husband, only she and Zack knew.

There were lessons to learn from all experiences, and Zack came to his own conclusions from his parents' failed marriage. If a man chose to lead a certain kind of life, a life high on personal fulfillment and low on safety and security, he had no business taking on long-term responsibilities. If nothing else, Zack's childhood had taught him the futility of trying to be something or someone he wasn't. In many ways Zack believed he bore a strong resemblance to his father. He loved life in the fast lane, loved never knowing what would happen when he turned the next corner. He made a difference in the world or tried to. Still, unlike his father, he never did things halfway. He wasn't willing to

give a woman half his heart, half his time or half his attention. He thought of it as the eleventh commandment: Thou
shalt not marry. If he couldn't promise forever, he would
make no promises at all.

And so he usually went home alone at night, ordered his
meals brought in and sent his laundry out. He had no trouble
avoiding women who might be vulnerable, spending what
little spare time he had with lovely ladies who knew the
score long before he had come along. He made sure he
treated them very well, and never stayed around long
enough for any complications to arise. He figured if he could
come into the world and leave the world without breaking
anyone's heart in between, he would be content.

This time, however, things were different. He was the one
wishing for more while the lady bade him goodbye and left
him where he stood. It seemed there were a few surprises
left in life, after all.

He sat up and turned the bedside radio on, finding a
golden-oldies station. He pumped up the volume, surrendering himself to a night of mournful love songs and re-
frigerated air.

Before her unexpected incarceration in the basement of
Appleton's, Anna had planned to do a bit more driving that
night. Now, however, it was well after midnight and hard
to come up with the motivation to drive when she didn't
quite know where she was going. Not to mention the fact
that her highly emotional encounter with Zack Daniels
seemed to have robbed her of all her energy. She found an
all-night convenience store and picked up some chocolate-
covered graham crackers, milk and red licorice for a belated
dinner, then decided to find a motel.

It didn't take long for her to realize Providence wasn't
exactly a hot spot for tourists. She could find only one motel, and when Anna roused the manager with the bell on the
front desk, the older woman practically growled at her.

Anna apologized for disturbing her rest, though her sincerity was seriously in question. She wasn't worried about disturbing a grouchy motel manager. She was worried she had done the wrong thing by leaving Zack Daniels in the parking lot where he stood. No telephone numbers had been exchanged, and there was no way for them to meet again in more normal circumstances. Still, she knew it was the safest thing to do. She had her life, he had his, and they had nothing in common besides being locked in a basement one night. Logic told her that brooding about Zack was a waste of time. Her emotions, however, felt a little bruised and tender and completely refused to back up the logic. One kiss, and suddenly she was a stranger to herself.

Once in her room, she realized she had never purchased the medicine she had gone into Appleton's for in the first place. Throughout the past two weeks, her stomach had been on a nonstop roller coaster. For one thing, she had never enjoyed being away from home. Her home and her friends were her security, and she was happiest when surrounded by the things and the people she loved. Unfortunately, a vacation of sorts had suddenly become necessary. One of her oldest and dearest friends, Kyle Stevens, was engaged to marry a lovely woman named Carrie. Anna had been thrilled for both of them, until one painful evening when Kyle had showed up on her doorstep, bright-eyed drunk, and revealed secret feelings for Anna that were anything but platonic. His timing was particularly bad, as his wedding was less than a month away. Anna truly believed his fascination for her was nothing more than a case of last-minute jitters. Kyle was a thirty-nine-year-old veterinarian who had never been married. He worked with animals all day who were remarkably undemanding, so suddenly sharing his life with a woman would probably be a huge adjustment. Anna wasn't surprised he'd come down with a bad case of tootsie frostbite. Still, she knew it would be best if she took herself out of the equation until just before the wedding. She had fabricated a story about visiting an old friend from her college days in San Francisco and embarked upon a very sudden vacation. Since there *was* no old friend, it was a boring and extremely lonely vacation. Hence, the angry eruption from her stomach. Hence, the stop in Providence for Tums.

Instead of Tums, she got Zack Daniels. Oh boy, did she.

She told herself to get a grip on her wistful thoughts. To take her mind off the man, she called her number in Grayland Beach to check any messages. She found there were four messages, each and every one from Kyle.

"We've got some things to talk about, Anna. Please call when you get this message."

"I still haven't heard from you. I'm getting married in two weeks. What am I supposed to do?"

"This isn't very nice of you. We have to talk, Anna."

"Anna, none of us have heard from you. When you get this message, *call*."

Anna slapped her hand on her forehead, blowing out an exasperated breath. It was too late now to return the calls. She had hoped that he would have come to his senses by now, but it seemed he was still demented. She had been completely honest with him before she left, telling him firmly they were only friends, but he didn't seem to be getting the message. Anna loved Kyle's fiancée, Carrie, almost as much as she loved Kyle, and the last thing she wanted to do was to hurt her. What on earth was she going to do? Now it seemed Kyle was thinking of postponing things unless she went home. She was damned if she did and damned if she didn't.

She changed into an oversize T-shirt, then crawled beneath the covers. Sleep, however, seemed to be a long way off. She found herself reliving the events of that evening over and over, particularly the bone-melting kiss. When her body began wriggling beneath the sheets, she decided this was doing her no good whatsoever. She sat up in bed and flicked on the bedside lamp, then occupied herself by staring at the blank television screen and twiddling her thumbs. She'd spent the past thirteen nights in lonely hotel rooms, but never one that felt quite as empty and lonely as this one.

Suddenly from the room upstairs came the mournful strains of an old Righteous Brothers tune. The floors of the motel must have been paper thin, as it sounded like Bill and Bobby were standing right there in the room with her. Still, it was a pleasant distraction, and she was in the perfect mood for a melancholy love song. It felt as though Zack was still with her, nudging her emotions, tantalizing her body, teasing her with his sensual appeal.

She wondered where he was.

Zack took his own sweet time showering and dressing in the morning, as he had nowhere in particular to go and nothing to look forward to when he got there. He attempted to call in Anna's license plate number, but he happened to get the one and only dispatcher who had a grudge against him. Zack had unknowingly taken out the fellow's girlfriend once, and the guy just couldn't get over it. He refused to run the check for no other reason than, "Hell hasn't frozen over yet, Daniels."

Zack decided he'd wait till his buddy Will was in the office and ask him to run the plate. In the meantime he was hungry. He checked out of the motel, threw his gear in the Lotus and quickly decided to walk down the street to McDonald's. Somehow he couldn't see driving his eye-catching bullet car into Ronald McDonald's parking lot. The Lotus and Ronald didn't blend.

The sky was clear and the sun was drying up the puddles on the street. Zack's mood, however, remained cloudy. He was hoping a couple of Egg McMuffins would cheer him up a little. He had a thing for Egg McMuffins, and he needed all the cheer he could get right now. His vacation had gone from really bad to downright rotten.

Due to his cop training, Zack had developed a habit of

scanning an entire room when he entered. McDonald's was bustling—mothers with kids, kids by themselves, teenagers who might as well be kids judging by the noise they made. And way in the back of the store in the brightly painted Playplace were even more kids, running over, under and on top of slippery slides, carousels and teeter-totters like streams of army ants.

Zack's semi-bored gaze skimmed over the action in the Playplace, then abruptly froze. There was a young woman sitting at one of the tiny tables, watching the boisterous children and ignoring the food on the tray in front of her. She was in profile, the most picture-perfect profile Zack had ever seen. Tiny nose, stubborn chin, luscious, man-killer lips. A curtain of glossy honey-gold hair completely hid the back of the bright yellow chair she sat on. She was dressed simply, in soft blue jeans and a white tailored shirt rolled up at the elbows. A silver bracelet glinted on her wrist. Her expression was remote, as if deep in thought.

Hot-diggity-dog, Zack thought gleefully. At that moment, a monsoon could have swept through Providence, Oregon, and Zack's smile would have come through shining.

He ordered his multiple Egg McMuffin breakfast, keeping an eye on the siren in the Playplace. Tray in hand, he made his way through the "adult" section of the restaurant, heading straight for an empty chair at Anna's table. He sat down as if he owned the place, and her electric eyes widened.

"You?" she croaked. As it happened, she had been thinking about him at that very moment, and apparently her thoughts had actually conjured him. Holding him in her gaze again made her senses jump to attention.

"Did you miss me?" he asked cheerfully, suddenly at peace with the world. "You know what they say about really good-looking men, don't you? They're hard to get rid of."

Anna's smile started in her eyes and spread to her lips. She couldn't help it. By nature, she was not an unhappy

person, and seeing him again had just put an end to her
rather melancholy reverie. She had no choice but to enjoy
this little gift of fate. "At least this time, we've got a way
out," she said, nodding toward the exit doors. "And the
walls are all glass, so I won't be passing out on you, either.
Aren't you relieved?"

She looked good in the morning, Zack thought. *Really*
good. Her eyes were a fresh summer blue, her sun-streaked
hair gleamed, and her pristine, button-down shirt was a
beautiful contrast against her lightly tanned skin. He'd seen
his share of women who didn't look so good first thing in
the morning. Hair flattened, makeup smeared, they would
scramble to a mirror to "put their faces on." Zack had always found that a frightening statement. He feared waking
up in the night and finding a faceless woman at his side.

Anna would be different. She had a natural beauty that
didn't rely on cosmetics for artificial enhancement. He could
imagine her waking up in bed, opening her sleepy eyes and
turning to him, smiling a lazy, brand-new-day hello. *And*
she would have a face, he had absolutely no doubt.

"Um...what was the question?" he asked stupidly,
knowing she'd asked him something, but distracted by his
PG-13 fantasy. "My mind went out for a walk just then.
You asked...?"

"If you were relieved...?"

"To see you?" He nodded his head enthusiastically.
"Monumentally."

"No." She wrinkled her nose at him. "To know you
aren't trapped in here with me."

"Oh." Always quick on the uptake, he switched gears
immediately, shaking his head with sorrow. "No, that
doesn't relieve me at all. It means I'll have to come up with
a new way of holding you captive. Still, I'm sort of a creative kind of guy. I've always admired that about myself.
I'll think of something. It's a darn shame I didn't bring my

handcuffs along. You never know when they'll come in handy."

Anna found it impossible to keep from laughing. Zack Daniels was the most disarming man she had ever met, full of teasing humor and unabashedly admiring. It was as if he had a permanent candle lit up inside, and she could feel the warm brightness pulling her in whenever she looked into his eyes. He had the remarkable ability to captivate with an irrepressible, lighthearted charm, while at the same time remaining every inch a very adult male. Anna figured there would be a large army of women only too happy to get locked up in a basement with him. Forever. "I still can't believe my intuition failed me when I tried to guess what you did for a living. You fit the policeman mold perfectly. Did your work bring you up here?"

Zack shrugged. "Sort of. My partner and I got caught up in a little ruckus during a drug bust. The dealer got mad."

Anna leaned her elbows on the table and her chin on her hands. She was fascinated by his matter-of-fact way of talking about such a dramatic situation. "That's it? He got mad?"

He opened his gray eyes innocently. "Wouldn't you?"

"So what happened? Are you hiding from him or something?"

Zack paused unwrapping his first Egg McMuffin to sniff indignantly. "As if I would. The dealer wounded my partner. When he did that, he dropped to the bottom of the food chain. If I knew what rock he'd crawled under, I sure as hell wouldn't be hiding from him. We got a couple of the peons, but the head honcho got away. Captain Todd—you remember, I mentioned him last night? Well, Captain Todd in his infinite wisdom decided I needed to be invisible till things cooled down. Actually, until *I* cooled down. He didn't want me killing people hither and yon. So, do you know what he did? You won't believe this. He forced me to take my *vacation*."

Anna blinked. "That's it? You're upset because he made you take a vacation?"

"I hate vacations." Zack's sunny expression was back in a heartbeat. "At least, I *used* to hate vacations. Since last night things have changed. I love vacations now. I love Captain Todd now. He's going in my will. Without him I wouldn't have met you."

Anna had never been compared to a drug bust before. Still, his meaning was unmistakable. She was flustered, buying herself a little time to regroup by tearing open little packets of sugar and dumping them into her coffee. "That's so weird. You were mad at Captain Todd because he was looking after your best interests?"

"That's not the *only* reason I was mad. I work in Los Angeles, California. And not the pretty part of Los Angeles, mind you. I don't know how long my vacation's going to be, but I can guarantee the law will be broken a few thousand times while I'm gone." Zack sighed wistfully. "I've had a lot of experience on the streets and I'm usually pretty handy to have around. I hate the feeling of not being there if I'm needed. Everybody thinks of southern California as kind of an extended Disneyland where fantasies are fulfilled and everyone is very tan with gleaming perfect teeth and two convertibles in every garage. It's just not that way."

"I know," Anna said with a shrug of her shoulders. "I lived in Los Angeles until I was twelve. I've never been to Disneyland, but I imagine L.A. doesn't even come close."

Zack was encouraged. She was relaxing and revealing more about herself, which was exactly what he wanted. "I didn't think there was a kid in the world who lived in southern California and never visited Disneyland."

"I was raised in foster homes," Anna said matter-of-factly, "and trips to Disneyland weren't top priority. When I was adopted, my parents lived in Grayland Beach, Oregon. I've spent the majority of my life up there. And believe me,

I wasn't deprived. I had such a great life in Grayland Beach, I never wanted to go anywhere else."

Zack stared at her, the soft heat of anger filling his chest. He tried to visualize her as a child, tried to imagine what it had been like for her. He wished he hadn't had so much experience with foster homes. He might have been able to convince himself it hadn't been too bad for her. Yet amazingly, there wasn't a shred of self-pity in her voice. Her extravagant eyes lit up when she talked about her adoptive parents, and he knew she had found unconditional love. She'd beaten the statistics, being adopted at twelve years of age. Quietly he said, "I'm happy it turned out well for you."

"Better than well," Anna said. "I was one of the lucky ones."

Zack dredged up a smile. "You're also one of the amazing ones. Gorgeous *and* lucky."

There he went again, catching her off guard with his sexy smile and lavish charm. Anna went back to her sugar packets. Rip, dump, toss. Rip, dump, toss. "Have you ever noticed that the most beautiful things in the world are also the most useless, like ice sculptures and peacocks? Beauty is highly overrated."

"Anna?"

She ripped open another packet. "Yes, Mr. Policeman?"

He bit his lip, but not hard enough to kill his grin. "Your coffee is pretty well sweetened. You've created a Mount McSugar in that cardboard cup."

Anna looked at the coffee spilling over the sides of her cup, then rolled her eyes and slumped in her seat. It seemed that even the most innocent contact with Zack Daniels turned her into an instant airhead. What on earth had happened to her usual personality? Granted, for the first time in her life she had encountered a man who was capable of getting under her skin, but that hardly merited instant schizophrenia. Anna wasn't a gun-toting cop, but she did enjoy living every moment of life to the fullest, as Zack obviously did. Her "potentially hazardous situation" radar was up and flashing neon red. All right, so she was vulnerable to a knowing smile, magnetic personality and a talented pair of lips. Who wouldn't be? "I'm not usually like this," she muttered, shaking her head. "Still, I guess you're probably used to it."

Zack took a bite of his Egg McMuffin. Ahh, ambrosia. "Used to what?"

"Women acting like dimwits around you. You're a walking dream."

Zack started to choke. Alarmed, Anna jumped up and started slapping him on the back—hard—until he grabbed her hand. "Stop it, woman! You're going to crack a vertebrae. I'm not dying, I was just shocked. I can breathe now. Sit. I'm paralyzed from the waist down, but other than that, I'm fine."

Anna returned to her yellow plastic seat with a cheerful smile. "What do you mean, shocked? Hasn't a woman ever drooled over you before?"

Zack regarded her incredulously. "This is completely unacceptable. Women shouldn't fluster men. That's encroaching on the male's territory."

"Just because I said—"

"Cut it out! I swear you say anything that comes into your mind. What's the matter with you?"

"Honesty is scary?"

"No, but some discretion is necessary. You can't go around willy-nilly, just speaking your mind."

Anna lifted her chin in the air. "And why not?"

"Because relationships between men and women are sort of like a game. You know, like Candyland for grown-ups. There are rules to the game. I am the one who flusters, you are the one who *gets* flustered. Tarzan brave, Jane gorgeous and flustered. It's the way of the world."

"That's such a crock. You're a chauvinist, Mr. Police-man."

He grinned with great satisfaction. "Thank you. And you are a remarkable woman, one whose like I have never seen. If only we could have stayed locked in that basement for the entire two weeks of my vacation, I would have absolutely nothing to complain about."

He was flirting again, but she couldn't help the unwilling grin that broke over her face. "Well, I sympathize. I've just been forced to take a vacation of sorts myself, and I was constantly bored, not to mention..." Her voice trailed off. She stared at Zack until he actually looked over his shoulder to see if some large predatory animal was sneaking up on him.

"What?" he asked, spooked. "Blink or something, will you?"

"I...have...an...idea," she said slowly, still glassy-eyed. "The most *outrageous* idea. Zack...you could very well be the answer to my prayers."

"Oh, I like this idea already," Zack replied happily. Anything to keep her sitting across from him as long as possible. McDonald's had never possessed such magical ambiance before. "Tell me. I'm all ears."

Anna hesitated, wondering if this was absolutely insane on her part. What she was about to propose could result in some rather serious complications if she didn't keep her wits about her. If nothing else, she had discovered she was particularly susceptible to off-duty cops with charm to spare. Still, she wasn't a child. She had always managed to accomplish her goals by remaining heart-whole and stubbornly optimistic. Her adoptive parents had always stressed the importance of smiling cheerfully through the ups and downs of life. There was no reason to think she couldn't pull this off without becoming personally involved.

"This will sound pretty wild," she said slowly, "and it is, actually. But I have this little problem waiting for me at home, and I think you might be able to help me with it. We've just met, and you might think I'm being too forward—"

"If you knew me better, you wouldn't say that. Go on."

Anna started drawing finger circles on the tabletop. "Well...I have this friend, Kyle. He's a veterinarian in Grayland Beach. Have I mentioned him before?"

Zack gave a long-suffering sigh. "You've mentioned several of your male friends to me. But no, I believe this is the first I've heard of Kyle the veterinarian. I can't imagine how on earth you keep all these men straight in your head. Go on, I'm all ears."

"Well, we've known each other for eons and we've always been really close, but he went wacko on me a couple of weeks ago. We were going over some things for the wedding one evening—"

"Beg pardon?" Zack sat up like a puppet whose strings had just been yanked skyward. "How close? How wacko? *Whose* wedding?"

"*Kyle's* wedding," Anna explained, wondering what on earth had put the fire in Zack's storm-colored eyes. "He's engaged to marry a really sweet girl named Carrie. She's very thoughtful and kind, and they're truly perfect for each other."

Zack instantly relaxed. "Oh, that's good. I've always liked Carrie."

"You don't know Carrie," Anna said.

"That's irrelevant. Go on, I'm on the edge of my seat."

Two Egg McMuffins later, Zack knew it all. The way Anna had first met Kyle thirteen years earlier, when her father had been the coach of the high school football team. Then Kyle had left for school and Anna hadn't seen him for several years. When he'd come home to open his veterinary practice years later, he'd stopped by and visited Carson Smith. Anna was all grown-up by that time, and they had instantly become fast friends. At this point Zack's eyes had started to narrow. When he heard the part about Kyle confessing his feelings to Anna, he almost lost his Egg McMuffin. Still, he managed to hear it all without comment, nodding understandingly in all the right places.

"So, let me sum this up," he said finally, folding his arms on the tabletop. "Your good friend Carrie—who, by the way, seems to be the only female in the entire world you are acquainted with—is supposed to marry your good friend Kyle. Only Kyle, who in my opinion sounds like a devious scoundrel—"

"He is not a scoundrel, nor is he devious."

"That's your opinion. Devious Kyle is suffering from wedding jitters and is distracting himself with thoughts of his beautiful best friend, *you*. And, being the wonderful girl you are, you attempted to defuse the situation by taking a little vacation of your own. Obviously, you want to go home as soon as you can, but Kyle the insensitive numbskull—"

"Why do you keep insulting a man you don't even know?"

"Don't interrupt, I'll lose my train of thought. Ding-dong Dr. Kyle is showing no signs of coming to his senses. You're afraid if you *do* go home, he'll cancel the wedding, and you're afraid if you *don't* go home he'll cancel the wedding. Have I missed anything?"

"Yes," she replied promptly. "*Your* part in all this."

"I didn't know I had a part, but I'm excited to hear it. I hate feeling useless. Please go on."

"Well, it has occurred to me that you don't seem to have anything really important to do for a few days, so maybe you could…help me out." Anna took a deep breath, then plunged in. "I'd like you to come home with me and pretend you love me."

Four

Zack had heard all kinds of propositions throughout the course of his career. Not a one had the nuclear-bomb effect of this particular proposition.

"You want me to go home with you?" he asked stupidly. Then, a bit louder, "And pretend I love you? Is that what you said?"

"Well, don't look so shocked. You won't be in any mortal danger, or anything. The key to the whole thing is *pretend*. For heaven's sake, you're a cop. I thought you were used to unusual situations." Then, after a short pause, "You've never been this quiet for this long. Are you still breathing?"

Zack realized he wasn't, and immediately rectified the matter. "I'm not shocked," he gasped, pulling oxygen into his paralyzed lungs. "I've been around, you know. It takes a lot to shock me. It's just…it's just…"

"It's just what?"

I've never had a dream come true before. "You took me

by surprise, that's all. I'm not often on the receiving end of this sort of proposition. I'm…collecting my thoughts.''

Anna stared at him, feeling the hot sting of blood in her cheeks. She knew her suggestion was a little outrageous, but he seemed to like her. And he obviously needed a bit of entertainment to take his mind off all the crime he was missing back in Los Angeles. It was an ideal situation, where they could both help each other out. "I realize you don't really know me, and I probably sound crazy as a loon. But don't you think it's strange that we met up when we were both suffering because of unwanted vacations? And then locked up in a basement together? It seems like we were destined to meet, don't you think?''

Zack nodded enthusiastically. "Oh, yes. Absolutely. I'm a big believer in destiny.''

"You see? It's perfect. If you could stay with me just a few days, until Kyle and Carrie get married, it would help me out tremendously. You see, he doesn't really love me, not in *that* way. He's just been a bachelor for so long that the closer the wedding gets, the more excuses he's coming up with to cancel it.''

"You know," Zack ventured, "there *are* those men who are fairly certain they wouldn't make good husbands. It's a good thing to realize that before you get married, don't you think?''

"Kyle's not like that at all," Anna replied promptly. "He and Carrie are soul mates, I'm certain of it. That's why our little charade would work. Deep down he loves Carrie with all his heart. Losing her would utterly destroy him.''

"Well, I'd hate for Kyle to be utterly destroyed. At least, I think I would.''

"Besides, you'd have a freebie vacation in Grayland Beach—it's a great seaside town, full of tourists. You could swim or go fishing or read…do whatever off-duty policemen like to do. Best of all, I could go home. If we play our parts well, Kyle would believe I was smitten with you, he'd realize what really mattered to him, and everyone would live happily ever after. It's perfect.''

Yes, it is, Zack thought happily. *There is such a thing as a heaven, and its name is Grayland Beach.* Suddenly his vacation had a different spin on it. Best of all, it was a short-term situation, so there would be no time for emotional complications. They would be serving each other's purposes very well.

Still, he couldn't appear too eager. "There is the matter of my virtue, you know," he said solemnly. "Sharing a home with a near-stranger, and all that.''

"Oh, that's funny. Really funny. I'm the one taking the risk here, and if I feel pretty safe, you probably should. If it will make you feel better, I'll cross my heart and promise not to compromise you.''

"Oh." There was a wealth of exaggerated disappointment in the little word. "How reassuring.''

"We have a deal?''

Zack grinned, resisting the urge to turn cartwheels in the Playplace. "I'm tickled to death to be of service. After all, I have sworn to protect and serve the people of California. You're from Oregon, but since you once lived in Los Angeles, I'll make an exception this time and serve you, as well." He played that back in his mind and added, "It would be a strictly platonic service, of course. On my best behavior at all times, unless someone is looking.''

"This is wonderful," Anna breathed, her eyes lighting up. "You'll do it? I can actually go home?''

"Yes, and I can actually go with you." Zack was dumbstruck by his own good fortune. He couldn't have planned this any better himself. "I feel like I'm taking advantage of you, to tell you the truth. After all, I'm getting free room and board.''

"It's the least I can do for you helping me out. All you'd have to do is back me up. Play the part, pretend we're smitten with each other. I'm certain that would help Kyle realize how important Carrie really is to him. This way Kyle and I will still be friends when this is all over."

"I'm happy I can help you and Dr. Doolittle *just* be friends," Zack said magnanimously. "Besides, it gives me something to do." Something very sweet, his own personal Mount McSugar. "Now, about the rest of your male friends. If you want Kyle to swallow this, you can't be spending any time with anyone else. *No other men.* No more Davy or Frank, not while I'm there. We have to make this look good. Agreed?"

"Of course."

"Do you think you can convince Kyle you're absolutely, completely, positively infatuated with me? It would require some serious acting on both our parts. *Serious* acting."

"When Kyle's around," Anna qualified.

"Well, of course when Kyle's around. There would be no point to acting all googly-eyed when he's not around, would there?" Zack rubbed his hands together with great anticipation. He loved a challenge, and from what he knew of Anna Smith, he was certain this would be an exceptionally enjoyable challenge. "This will be fun. Undercover cops are very good at acting, you know. We're always having to bluff our way through sticky situations."

"Well, that's encouraging," Anna said doubtfully. "I'm sure I don't have as much practice acting as you do, but I'm a quick study."

Zack smiled. Smoothly he said, "I'm a good teacher."

"I'll just bet you are. Well…" Anna stood up, clearing up the cartons and napkins on the table. "I guess we can be on our way. The drive isn't too long, only a few hours from here. I've absolutely hated being away from home. I didn't sleep at all last night. You have no idea how happy I'll be to get into my own bed."

"Well then, I guess we just became partners in crime. So to speak." Zack stood up as well, wanting to hit the road before she had a chance to reconsider. "It seems like the same things keep happening to us. I didn't sleep a wink myself last night, then this morning we both head to McDonald's for breakfast. Fate is definitely playing a part here."

"Fate," Anna said firmly, "is what you make it. I learned that a long time ago."

Zack grinned at her, feeling very kindly toward a benevolent fate at that moment. "If you say so."

"It's true. You can't leave anything to chance in this life. You've got to make the most of every day, every minute."

Zack's sparkling eyes took in her swinging hair, the snug fit of her jeans, the way she wrinkled her turned-up nose when she tried to make a point. "I intend to, Anna. From this second on."

There was something about being closely followed for three hours by a car that looked as though it came straight from the Grand Prix that was detrimental to Anna's driving. Since she wasn't a good driver in the best of circumstances, this was bad. She repeatedly found herself weaving back and forth across the yellow line, exceeding the speed limit by as much as twenty-five miles an hour, and throwing up gravel and clouds of dust on the soft shoulder of the road when navigating S-curves. These things all happened when she paid more attention to her rearview mirror than to the road ahead of her.

The problem was the view. Some people would say the stretch of coastal road reaching into Oregon was one of the most picturesque trips one could take. But some people hadn't seen Zack Daniels driving a Lotus. As far as Anna was concerned, the man put Highway 105 to shame. He drove with the windows down, the wind softly beating his black hair around his California-tanned face. He also wore wraparound sunglasses that added to the exotic, elegant picture. Up until this point in her life, Anna had never understood women's susceptibility to a man driving a gleaming, undeniably sexy machine capable of breaking the sound barrier. And so, absentmindedly ignoring practically every rule of the road, she drove more than three hundred miles looking more behind her car than in front. It was a small miracle that she didn't wrap the Jeep around a tree. Once or twice she saw Zack toss one of his arms up in the air as if to say, *What the hell are you thinking?* But he stuck stubbornly behind her, never once losing sight. On reflection, she decided he probably had a lot of experience tailing people.

It was late afternoon when she pulled off the highway, happy to once again be traveling the familiar tree-lined streets of Grayland Beach. Her only regret was that Zack was seeing her beloved Victorian at this particular time of day. She had always felt that seeing a house for the first time was like meeting a person for the first time. It was important to be lively and memorable, while remaining true to one's individuality. When she first decided to restore the home she had lived in for so many years, she spent months researching the complicated color schemes, authentic materials and elaborate ornamentation of Victorian architecture. Then she set about interpreting them to suit her own unique personality. She had used seventeen shades of creamy pastels on the exterior of her home, a color scheme that had deeply offended the modern minimalist in her friend Davy. He had gone so far as to liken her home to a "color-blind peacock dressed to kill." Anna, however, was thrilled with the finished product. The fanciful towers and turrets of the Victorian reminded her of a fairy-tale castle, a fitting setting for Rapunzel, Sleeping Beauty or Anna Smith. She adored the stark-white gingerbread trim, expansive bay windows and deep wraparound porch which added to the charm. Granted, the rainbow of colors was a little unsettling to some of her neighbors, but Anna considered her "Painted Lady" a masterpiece of artistic creativity.

Unfortunately, with the sunlight slanting in from the west, the seventeen shades of paint she had so lovingly applied took on a startling brilliance that actually hurt one's eyes. It would have been better had she introduced Zack to her pride and joy in the soft light of morning, when the colors were mellowed and radiantly honeyed. It was a bit less intimidating that way. It was strange how very much she wanted Zack to like her masterpiece. She had put her heart and soul into every brush stroke, every bit of gold-leafing, each elaborate doodad and ornament. Her home provided tremendous insight into her secret hopes and dreams, standing proud for all the world to see.

She parked her car in the circular drive, her fingers shaking just a bit with nervousness. She got out and leaned against the car door, waiting as Zack's silver beast purred up behind. In the space of a heartbeat, he turned off the engine and climbed out of the car, staring her down for a full thirty seconds. Surprisingly he gave no impression of even seeing the attention-grabbing Victorian.

"Are you insane?" he asked.

Anna could see by looking into his eyes that this was not a rhetorical question. The man sincerely wanted an answer.

"Of course I'm not insane," she said indignantly. "Why? Just because of the colors? If you can't understand someone wanting to be original—"

"What colors?" Zack barked. "Are you talking about this *house?* I don't care what color your house is. Do you realize I should have arrested you about fifty times on the way up here?"

"What on earth are you talking about?"

"I'm talking about your *driving,* and I use the term loosely. Do you realize how much time you spent on the wrong side of the road? How on earth have you stayed alive this long?"

"Oh. My driving. Well, I like my driving to be original, too. Stop being an officer of the law for two minutes, you're on vacation." She thought it was a very good time to dis-

tract him. She pushed away from the car, wiping her palms
on her pants. "So, anyway, tell me what you think of
my—"

"Oh, no. You're not getting off that easy. What got into
you? I would have pulled alongside you and told you to
slow the hell down, but I was too scared to get that close."
For the past three hours Zack Daniels had experienced
something completely new in his life: fear, razor-sharp and
cutting-edge deep. Up until this point in his life, he'd never
truly been afraid of anything. He had known Anna Smith
for barely twenty-four hours, but the possible consequences
of her crazed NASCAR driving were anathema to him. How
dare she risk her life by not paying attention to the rules of
the road? Zack had never been one to get overly excited
about motor vehicle transgressions, but right now he was
way past "overly excited." Yesterday he had discovered
her. Today he could have lost her. "Just please tell me you
don't drive like that all the time. Tell me you went tem-
porarily insane or something. You have no idea how much
better that would make me feel."

"Listen, I don't drive like that all the time," Anna muttered, unwilling to tell him why she had been so distracted.
"I was just…excited to come home. We're going to change
the subject now. How do you like my house? And before
you answer, I want you to know that I restored it all by
myself, top to bottom."

Zack sighed deeply—it seemed he was doing a lot of that
lately—and took his first really good look at Anna's home.
The setting was perfect—tree-lined streets, sprinklers chug-
ging away on every other lawn, a couple of kids playing
basketball in the adjoining driveway. But the house itself
was a sight to see, something he'd never seen the like of
before. Right off the bat he flinched with the shock of all
those colors, then he pulled himself together and studied the
house with the eye of a trained observer. His gaze roamed
over the exotic ornamentation, the lacy trims, the painted
flowers and birds on the stucco archways. He felt as if he

had stepped into a time warp, transporting him to a softer, gentler age. Anna was there in all the whimsical details, her vibrant beauty and individuality reflected in the vivid colors and the imaginative flourishes. This was a house that had a delightful personality, and that personality was every bit as fascinating, imaginative and unique as Anna was herself.

She's a wonder, he thought to himself.

"It's truly amazing," he said quietly. He turned his attention back to Anna, a smile shaping his lips into the sweetest curve. "It's you," he said simply.

There was no sarcasm or artificial flattery in his tone, something Anna picked up on immediately. She had taken an enormous amount of teasing because of her enthusiastic restoration job. No one these days seemed to appreciate a truly creative endeavor...except for this remarkable man with hair as dark as a raven's wing and the most appealing smile she had ever seen. "You really do like it, don't you? I have to tell you that none of my friends appreciated my interpretation of genuine Victoriana. In fact, Kyle thinks I might be color-blind. He wants me to get an eye test."

"The more I hear about the man, the less I like him," Zack said. He strolled toward Anna, hands pushed carelessly into the pockets of his leather jacket. His smile stayed, growing sweeter with every step. "It's fairly obvious that Kyle doesn't get it."

Anna cleared her throat, his nearness kicking her pulse into what she had come to think of as Zack-rhythm. "Kyle doesn't get what?"

"This house is a wonderful background for you," he said, his silvery eyes delving softly, deeply into her. "Whimsical, appealing and unforgettable. Anyone with half a brain could see you belong here."

"What do you know?" Anna murmured, shaking her head. "You're a romantic. Very possibly the only romantic law-enforcement officer in existence. I'm honored to have you here, Mr. Romantic Policeman. And I sincerely appreciate your appreciation of my home.''

Zack was deeply embarrassed and decided to give her something else to think about. He stepped even closer, his soft, deep-set eyes beguiling. He reached out his hand, brushing the back of his knuckles against her cheek. ''You know, if we're determined to fool your buddy Kyle, we should—''

Without warning, the lovely moment crashed to earth with a jarring *thud*.

Oddly, neither of them had heard the sound of a car's engine. One moment, they were alone with a watercolor sunset and a rainbow Victorian. The next moment there were three of them in the picturesque setting: Zack, Anna and a tall fellow with a thundercloud in his face getting out of a Ford truck.

''An unexpected visitor dropping in on us,'' Zack said, raising his voice to be clearly heard by the new arrival. Normally people weren't able to sneak up on him quite like this. It was a good thing he was on vacation and not on duty. He was losing his edge. ''Hello, unexpected visitor. Who might you be?''

Kyle barely nodded to Anna, all his attention focused curiously on Zack. ''Funny, I was just about to ask that myself. I haven't met you before.''

''Well then, this must be your lucky day, buddy,'' Zack replied with cloying sweetness. ''Something tells me you're Kyle.''

Kyle gave him a stiff little smile. ''In the flesh. You have the advantage of me.''

''You're quick, Kyle, picking up on that already. I like a good loser.''

''Oh, dear.'' Anna realized this was rapidly getting out of hand, and the two men hadn't even been formally introduced. She stepped between them with a stiff, painted-on smile, feeling like she had just planted herself in the middle of a minefield. "Let's start over. Kyle, this is Zack Daniels. Zack, meet my friend Dr. Kyle Stevens. He's a veterinarian in Grayland Beach. I told you about him."

After a pregnant pause the men shook hands briefly. "Pleasure," Kyle said, his eyes conveying another message altogether.

"Delightful." Zack looked the man over, wishing Kyle had been really short or really overweight. Unfortunately, he looked like a regular guy. His tanned features were full of expression, hinting at the intelligence of the man within. He was perhaps an inch taller than Zack, and moved with a grace unusual in such a large man. His curly brown hair *was* thinning a bit, which was nice. He also wore a yellow golf shirt so bright it almost hurt Zack's eyes to look at it. Zack had never sized up a man as competition before, since he'd never felt in the least bit threatened by anyone else. "Anna has told me all about you, Kyle. You're getting married soon, right? To a great girl named *Carrie*. You must be very much in love with *Carrie*."

Kyle took a step closer to Zack, his chin lifted defensively. "I don't know if you're *trying* to irritate me, but you're doing a real good job of it."

Zack showed his teeth in something that was supposed to be a smile. "Well, I'd ask you to step outside, but we are outside. Still, if you—"

"Now, stop it," Anna said sternly. She abandoned any hope of the men having a civilized, grown-up conversation. "Let's get the luggage inside. It's been a long trip, and it's getting late."

"*Too* late," Zack echoed, smiling as he met Kyle's stormy eyes.

Anna took Zack on a tour of her home while Kyle trailed behind like a loyal spaniel on guard. The interior of Anna's home was everything Zack knew it would be, true to its Victorian nature down to the smallest details. Like Anna, very genuine. The rooms weren't particularly large, but possessed a charm and warmth that was almost tangible. Stained-glass windows were abundant, filling the interior with a hazy rainbow of colors. The bow-windowed parlor impressed visitors with an enormous crystal chandelier hanging from a ten-foot ceiling. The flooring and wainscot walls were burnished mahogany, window treatments made of burgundy fabric trimmed with extravagant fringe and tassels. There were little statues, silk flowers and jeweled lamps everywhere, as well as elaborately carved upholstered furniture. The dining area and kitchen were also on the main floor, with a glass-enclosed porch at the rear of the house. A spiral wooden staircase led to the bedroom suites on the second floor, while the third floor was dedicated to Anna's "studio." Here Zack realized the complexity of the woman who was so fascinating to him. There were several canvasses propped on easels, a couple of bar stools, and shelves laden with paper, paints, chalk and turpentine. An overstuffed chair snuggled against a deep bay window that overlooked the sea, with floor-to-ceiling bookcases nearby. Several bedsheets covered the floor, protecting the lustrous mahogany.

Studying the paintings themselves, Zack found yet another surprise. Each and every one of the paintings was absolutely horrible, with no exception. He glanced warily at Anna, patently relieved to see an understanding smile lifting her lips. Obviously, she knew these weren't exactly masterpieces. "You didn't tell me you...try to paint."

"I haven't had time. I've only known you for one—" Anna paused, glancing at Kyle "—for one week. I figured we'd get to all this eventually. Actually, this is the way I let off pressure. If I had a bad day at school, or if something is bothering me, I come up here and splash a little paint around. It's very therapeutic."

"There's a lot I don't know about you yet," Zack murmured, eyeing her appreciatively. "You're just one surprise after another."

"Speaking of surprises, when did you two meet?" Kyle asked.

Before Anna could answer, Zack jumped right in. "We met the second day of her vacation. I felt like I'd known her all my life. Anna's very comfortable to be around."

"You're not telling me anything I don't know," Kyle replied. "I've known her for a lot longer than you have."

"But not as *well*," Zack shot back in a silky voice.

"Oh, will you two give it a rest?" Anna felt the first whimper of a headache. She'd known Kyle was going to be difficult when she returned home, but she hadn't realized Zack was going to do his very best to irritate him even further. When they were finally alone again, she planned on having a little talk with him about his very specific responsibilities in this charade. "Let's go see what's in the fridge for dinner, children," she said, heading for the staircase. "I can't promise much, but I'm hoping if you two are busy chewing you won't be able to growl at each other."

That wistful fantasy, however, was not to be.

Seated at the antique cherrywood table in the kitchen, they made a meal of fried eggs, quite literally the last bit of food in her refrigerator. If Anna had hoped the lack of a decent meal might inspire Kyle to politely take his leave, she was dead wrong. He seemed glued to his chair, trading barely disguised insults with Zack. Neither man was paying much attention to their hostess or to their fried eggs.

Headache thundering, Anna finally decided to call a "truce-or-else." She suddenly slammed her palms on the antique table hard enough to make the plates jump, looking from Zack to Kyle with mutiny in her eyes. "*Enough* already! You two are making me crazy. Why can't you be nice to each other? Why can't you be polite?"

"Probably," Zack ventured helpfully, "because I don't like him."

"What a coincidence," Kyle muttered.

Anna groaned, knuckling her tired eyes. "This must be what it feels like to have children who argue constantly. I hope you're both happy, because you've given me the granddaddy of all headaches and I probably won't ever have children, and it's all your fault. Why can't you two act your age? Actually, if you'd make an effort to act even *half* your age, I would be grateful."

Zack's smile fell off his face as he studied the weary bent of Anna's head. This little testosterone contest might be a kick for him, but Anna was obviously at the end of her rope. He pushed his chair back from the table and stood up, giving the top of her head a little pat. "You're right, kiddo. I'm sorry. I think I'll go outside and get my things, maybe take a little walk down on the beach. You two can catch up while I'm gone. Nice insulting you, Stevens. Let's do it again some time when the pretty lady isn't around." And he strode off, cheerfully whistling "There'll Be a Hot Time in the Old Town Tonight."

Kyle waited until he heard the front door slam, then turned on Anna. "What do you think you're doing? You can't bring some man home from your vacation like a souvenir you picked up. What's the matter with you? This guy could be *anybody.*"

"Well, as it turns out, this guy is very nice, so stop obsessing. Would it make you feel better if I told you Zack is a policeman?"

"No. He's still a stranger."

Anna avoided Kyle's eyes, looking down at one very cold fried egg that looked right back at her with its single yellow eye. "You know, when you think about it, an egg is not a pretty thing. It's the yolk that turns me off. Not very appetizing."

"Anna, if you're going to try and distract me, find a subject more interesting than egg yolks. We both know why you left. Now you come home with a shiny new boyfriend in tow, and I'm supposed to be happy? I know I was out of line when I told you how I felt about you. I should have talked to Carrie first, and I apologize for that. But that's no reason for you to immediately jump into another relationship.''

"What do you mean, *another* relationship?'' Anna was hurting, knowing she was close to losing the best friend she had in the world. He had been a wise and funny companion, a man completely without airs or pretense. Why did he have to ruin everything? "We don't have a relationship, Kyle. We're the very best of friends, but that's all we are. What you're doing isn't fair, not to Carrie and not to me. Besides, I like Zack. It hasn't gone any further than that, but I want to give this a chance and see what happens. One day maybe I'll be lucky enough to find the same thing you found with Carrie.''

Kyle stared out the window, his jaw set. "What am I supposed to say to that?''

Anna ignored his question. "How is Carrie? I hope you didn't tell her—''

"About my second thoughts?'' Kyle looked back at Anna, not even trying to hide the naked emotion in his eyes. "No. I wouldn't know what to say. I don't understand myself what's happening here.''

"Nothing is happening here,'' Anna said gently. "I love you like a brother. We'll always be friends.''

For a long moment he stared at her, a muscle ticking in his hard cheek. Then, without another word, he stood up and left. Anna watched him through the kitchen window walking toward his truck. His shoulders had a tired look, as if all the troubles in the world were resting there.

"Bye, Kyle,'' she whispered, tears misting her eyes.

Five

Zack was being a very good boy. At least, he *thought* he was being a very good boy. Judging by the way Anna was suddenly looking at him, she might have a different opinion.

She had led him to one of the bedrooms on the second floor, a large room with a fireplace, half-tester bed and private bath. It was definitely a ''girly'' room, with pale-rose walls, a cream-colored crocheted lace bedspread and matching draperies. Not wanting to hurt her feelings, he told her he would be more than comfortable here.

At that she'd smiled faintly, knowing he probably had never stayed in a pink bedroom in all his life. Then he'd made the mistake of asking where *her* room was. The question had been very polite and completely innocent, but Anna hadn't taken it that way.

''Why do you need to know where my room is?'' she asked.

Oh-oh, Zack thought, inwardly wincing at the suspicion in her eyes. *I'm on my best behavior here, but she isn't in a mood to believe it.* "Anna...I was just making conversation. Look, I'm sorry about the complications with your friend Kyle, but it isn't my fault. I'm just here to help."

"I know. I'm sorry." She was more than a little depressed, worrying about Kyle and the threat to their friendship. He was family. The thought that she was the source of his pain was deeply disturbing. "It's just...Kyle means a great deal to me. I lost my adoptive parents four years ago, and my friends became my family. I'm closer to Kyle than probably anyone else in the world. I couldn't bear losing him."

That was a double whammy for Zack. First she told him that she'd lost the family it had taken her so long to find, a bit of news that hit him in the stomach like a fist. How much should one person have to take, and where was her anger, her bitterness? She seemed to accept the loss with enormous grace and courage. Then she admitted to caring for Kyle a "great deal." Just how much was a great deal? Had he read her wrong? "Look, if you've changed your mind, if I'm more of a complication than a solution, I'll go. If you've decided you truly care for Kyle—"

"No," Anna told him quickly, shaking her head. "I mean, yes, but not in that way. Why on earth did he have to mess things up? We used to be the best of friends. Now...now I don't know what we are."

"Well," Zack said quietly, "if that's true, if you care for him just as a friend..."

She looked away, biting down hard on her lip. "He's just a friend. But a friend I don't want to lose," she said softly.

"Then I hope you won't misunderstand what I'm going to say. When you told me about Kyle, I didn't realize he was quite so hung up on you. The guy has it bad. Unless we do a better job of convincing him we're falling in love, his wedding isn't going to happen."

Falling in love. Hearing those simple words from Zack was surprisingly powerful, distracting her from her depressing reverie. Looking at Zack, she couldn't help but notice what a fetching picture he made, denim shirt hanging out over his jeans, the overhead light casting a deep-blue sheen over his black hair. There was a gentleness in his silvery eyes, along with something more personal she didn't want to examine too closely. He looked strong, enticing and dangerously masculine. Anna felt the tiny sparks of a moment's glance shiver up and down her spine. *I'm becoming a predatory woman,* she thought despairingly. *I should be ashamed.*

"I told you it was a pickle," she managed. "What else can I do?"

"Just pretend you care," Zack said very softly. This time there was no smile, no teasing, none of his customary humor. "About *me.* When you look at me, put your heart in your eyes. Act as if we're two human beings who love each other because we looked at each other."

Anna couldn't look away from his eyes. The silence became louder and louder, if such a thing was possible. Finally she whispered, "You're a romantic, Mr. Policeman."

"Believe me, I'm only romantic with the right inspiration."

She gave him a small, uncertain smile, then turned on her heel and walked out of the room, closing the door behind her.

Zack remained rooted to the spot for a long moment, staring at the door as if he could see Anna on the other side. His mind was going at warp speed. He was alone in the house with the most beautiful, intelligent and entertaining companion he had ever known. For a moment he let his libido off the leash, allowing it to revel in freedom. He happily fantasized about leaving his room in the deep of night, finding her standing in her bedroom doorway, waiting....

"Here, boy," he called aloud to his libido. Time to get a grip on his wishful, wonderful imagination. Anna's world was very complicated at the moment. Her old friend Kyle was suddenly looking at her with desire in his eyes. Her new friend Zack also looked at her with desire in his eyes. There was a wedding coming up and no one knew who was going to end up wedded to whom. Anything could happen.

And Zack loved the unpredictability of it all. This was almost as good as being back on the streets of Los Angeles looking for bad guys.

No, damn it…it was better.

Zack made a noble attempt to sleep in the girly bed, up to his nose in floral-scented sheets, his head lost in the midst of a half dozen lacy pillows. This was far different from the largely undecorated apartment he had kept in Los Angeles for nearly six years now. He simply wasn't home enough to worry about making a little nest for himself. He could have called in a decorator, but his buddies on the force would wonder where all the money came from for the new furnishings. Instead, he deliberately lived with an "early garage sale" motif, like most of the other unmarried cops. There had been the occasional girlfriend who had decided to save him from his spartan existence, showing up with vases of flowers and knickknacks for the coffee table. As they grew more comfortable, the refrigerator would suddenly fill to overflowing with orange juice, bacon, vegetables and milk. The appearance of the four food groups always signaled the beginning of the end for the relationship. Zack would gradually back off, the lady in question would find someone else to coddle and care for, and all would be right with his world. He was used to his bare walls, bare refrigerator and simple furniture. And his sheets were black cotton, which he considered very manly.

Tonight he was seriously out of his element in a tumble of pink lace and ivory crocheting. The shock had caused the sandman to "take a powder," as the boys said at the precinct. It seemed that meeting Anna Smith had somehow

transformed Zack into a permanent insomniac. His efforts
to sleep were futile and frustrating, as his mind was seriously obsessed with her proximity. Eventually he gave up,
wandering about the room and discovering interesting bits
of Victoriana. On a marble-topped curio table he found a
brass ostrich lamp he hadn't noticed before, a startling bit
of whimsy that gave him the willies. If he turned out the
lights, that bird just might come alive and hunt him down.
As he considered the ostrich's googly eyes, which seemed
to follow him about the room, a smile broke over Zack's
face. Wasn't bird anxiety a good reason to go in search of
some reassuring company?

Finding Anna would be wonderfully easy, as there were
muffled sounds coming from the third floor. He quickly
pulled on his jeans, then, barefoot and bare-chested, set off
to have an adventure. He figured Anna was probably working in her studio. It had been nearly two hours since she'd
left him alone with the spooky brass ostrich. He missed her
face.

At the top of the stairs, he realized she had soft music
playing. Zack had always been a sucker for classical guitar
music. Again, this was something he usually kept private.
One of these days he just might snap and turn into a schizophrenic, with all this hiding and pretending. If he'd chosen
to be anything else besides a cop, he might not have had to
worry quite so much about his reputation. Still, the satisfaction his job gave him put a respectable spin on the white
lies he told along the way.

The door to the studio was open. Zack saw Anna before
she saw him, which gave him a moment to take in the fascinating picture she made. She had changed into a paint-
splattered men's shirt and a pair of jeans ripped open at
both knees. She was barefoot, and her hair was tied up on
the top of her head in a loose ponytail. She was staring at
the painting on her easel while chewing thoughtfully on the
end of her paintbrush. Zack couldn't see much of the paint-

RYANNE COREY 81

ing itself, but he did notice the burst of radiant, eye-catching colors. He wasn't surprised. Her home, her art and the artist herself were all radiant and eye-catching.

"Beautiful picture," he said quietly, not referring to the painting.

Anna jumped, and the brush went flying. "Zack, you scared me to death. What are you doing still up? I thought you went to bed an hour ago."

He smiled. "I did. I just didn't go to sleep. You know that ostrich lamp in my room?"

"Yes…"

"It doesn't like me. Besides, I'm pining away for my work." It was yet another lie, but it *used* to be true. "I can't sleep when I'm pining. Do you always paint this late at night?"

"Actually, it's been a while since I've come up here. It's not a calling, it's just something I do when I'm bored or I need to work off excess energy. I can appreciate art—I just can't create it." As she looked at him leaning against the door frame, it occurred to Anna that she would like to paint him. It was a shame she had absolutely no talent whatsoever. She was fascinated with the miracles a brush could work on canvas; she simply wasn't much of a miracle worker herself. And so she dabbled, always amused by her own astonishing lack of creativity.

Had she the talent, however, Zack Daniels would have definitely been her next subject.

His body was beautifully defined, his bare, bronzed skin shimmering in the fluorescent lights. His heavy-lidded eyes shone like a deep, wild sea, inviting and unpredictable at the same time. In a logical corner of her mind Anna knew she was tired and worried about Kyle and Carrie, and her resources were low. It was very hard to fight physical attraction when she was taken by surprise like this. She bought herself some time by going after her paintbrush, which had rolled beneath the easel. "Did I disturb you? I'm not used to sharing the house with anyone, so I pretty much wander around at will. I'm sorry if I woke you up.''

"No, you're fine. I couldn't sleep, anyway, so I came to find you. Insomnia is always much more fun when you share it with someone.'' He slowly walked into the room, his eyes focused curiously on her painting. He saw a field of blinding yellow sunflowers with a bright Crayola rainbow arching above. A childish figure with corkscrew curls was half-buried in the flowers. ''Is that you?''

Anna gave a nervous little giggle, then quickly covered up the canvas with a sheet. ''No. I don't ever worry about who or what I paint. I just work out my frustrations up here. I've let very few people witness my extraordinary lack of talent. You just caught me off guard.''

"Good. That means we're even.'' When she stared at him curiously, his expressive mouth tucked up into a self-conscious, one-sided comma. ''You've been catching me off guard since the minute I saw you. And for your information, it's usually very difficult to throw me for a loop. I hope you're proud of yourself.''

"So tell me what else I don't know about you,'' Anna said. ''I know you're a cop, you play a killer game of chess and it's difficult for anyone to throw you for a loop. And that's pretty much all I know.''

Zack took his time answering. For whatever reason, he didn't feel like joking or teasing. Before he met Anna, he never worried too much about letting anyone know him. Life was less complicated that way, and he didn't like complications. Now, however, he found himself wanting her to understand him. ''There are a lot of things you don't know. I love reading. I like to pack up a tuna sandwich and take a book down to the beach. I don't like doing dishes, so I eat a lot of take-out Chinese out of the carton. I won my junior high school spelling bee. I'm knocked off my feet by a pair of beautiful blue eyes. Oh, and I hate veterinarians. It stems from a terrible childhood trauma. I had a poodle named Precious when I was a kid, and when I took it to the vet for her shots, she up and died from pure terror.''

"You're making up every word of that story,'' Anna accused him.

"Not the part about hating vets, I didn't,'' Zack threw right back, his eyes daring her to argue. "And it definitely stems from a trauma, and the trauma is named Kyle. Did I tell you that I didn't like him?''

She smiled a little. "You mentioned it. You don't seem to be the kind of man who keeps his emotions to himself.''

"Believe me,'' Zack said with feeling, "sometimes I *have* to keep my emotions to myself.''

He didn't bother to hide the look in his eyes that gave very intimate meaning to his words. For a moment they locked gazes, then Anna looked away, suddenly dry-mouthed and uncomfortable. She felt like a swimmer, holding her breath as she thrashed her way through the ocean in search of blue sky and life-giving oxygen. Everything within her was on pause. And she couldn't think of a thing to say.

"Did I make you nervous?'' he asked gently. "I'm sorry, I didn't mean to. Like you said, I'm not good at disguising my thoughts. But you can trust me. You know that by now, don't you?''

Her big eyes skittered to his face, yet avoided directly meeting his gaze. "We barely know each other.''

Zack waited until she finally met his eyes, a slight smile tipping his mouth. He took a step forward, standing so close to her that he could smell the faintest trace of her perfume. She also smelled like turpentine, and somehow the odd combination was sweetly endearing, every bit as unique as Anna herself. "You're right, Anna. We've known each other for only a little more than a day. I have no idea what your favorite color is, I don't know if you like red roses in a crystal vase or a big armful of wildflowers. I have no idea if you played with dolls when you were a kid, or if you were a tomboy with skinned knees. But I *do* know that your eyes are the same color as robins' eggs, and they dance when you smile. I know you chew on your lip when you're worried.'' An almost imperceptible pause. ''And I know that last night's kiss was magic.''

At that, she immediately bit down on her lip. Her gaze shimmered with a deep-water blue, softly unfocused and hypnotic. Zack was right, then: she did do that when she was nervous. Before she'd been reluctant to look in his eyes; now she couldn't look away. His words caught her straight in the heart. Last night *was* magic. And she knew from firsthand experience that magic was terribly hard to come by in the world.

''I know,'' she whispered. ''I know.''

He seemed to still. As he stared at her, he projected an unmistakable intensity that was as beguiling and powerful as the man himself. There was an immense appeal in the way his jeans hung precariously low around his narrow hips, in the smooth brown skin of his chest and the way his thick hair tangled across his forehead. The flat plane of his stomach was lean, hard and tight, each abdominal muscle very well-defined. Beneath her shirt, Anna's stomach also felt suddenly hard and tight, like a clenched fist. Her mouth went dry, and her eyelids felt curiously weighted. Drowsy-eyed, she forgot to hang on to her smile as her gaze spread like warm honey from his stomach to his chest. She was captivated by the erotic, shaded curves of bone and sinew, by the fluid, powerful muscles that enhanced his masculinity. And his lips—they were elegantly carved with the sweetest symmetry, the corners tipped permanently upward. His silvery eyes locked with hers, bottomless and dark, the outside edges framed with curling lines. His face carried the telltale signs of a lifetime of smiles, as well as the unmistakable dark glitter of sensual yearning.

Mesmerized, Anna felt herself tumble right into his eyes, falling as deep as she could go. She wasn't certain if she was floating up to him, or if he was drifting down to her, but they came together by slow, dragging inches. And when his lips closed gently over hers, she felt as if she was being fed after years of starvation. Her hands reached out instinctively for support, hands gliding over the satin-smooth flesh of his chest. She could feel the warm throbbing of his lifeblood beneath her palms, a rapid meter that matched her own hectic pulse.

His lips were deliciously coaxing, while at the same time sweetly hesitant. Strangely, Anna felt no need to control the situation, no fear he would try and take the kiss too far. Zack seemed just as tangled in unfamiliar emotions as she was. Her body felt ultrasensitive beneath the moist surface of her skin, and she truly felt she could almost taste him where they touched flesh to flesh. Her breasts felt lush with a delicious weight, softly aching to be touched. The first time this man had kissed her, the sensations had been impulsive, fiery and frantic, tinged with a forbidden recklessness. Anna had felt scorched when that first kiss was over, half-crazed by the intensity and surprise of it all. This time was so very different. He opened up his soul to her, revealing himself to be a gentle weaver of sensual spells that left her dazed. She thought she could feel pleasure tears behind her closed eyelids.

Magic. And all from a single kiss.

When Zack reluctantly broke from the kiss, his eyes were glazed with the soft heat of passion. He slowly lifted his hand, pulling at the small ribbon holding her hair. His expression was intense, as if he was completely mesmerized by this insignificant action. Anna's hair tumbled free in a weighted cloud over her shoulders and back. So feminine, so beautiful. Zack let the featherlight ribbon drop from his fingers, watching it float to the floor between them.

He surprised her then, slowly sinking to the floor on his haunches, hands dangling loosely between his legs as he tipped his head back to study her face. His gaze moved over her delicate features as if he had never seen her before. Her skin was flushed, her blue-sky eyes shining with sensuality and a woman's desire. Her luscious, wet-cherry lips were curved in a sweet, self-conscious smile. She made no effort to gloss over the moment until she had herself cool and composed. Zack found her simple honesty endearing. How many women had he known who deliberately disguised their emotions, to the point where they weren't sure themselves what they were feeling? Pride was more important than being candid and open.

Anna was different from anyone he'd ever met. She was still drifting, still breathless and shaky and reveling in it.

"Something's happening to us," he said quietly. His eyes were so dark, they had no color beyond the hectic glitter of sensuality. "Can you feel it?"

Anna tilted her head sideways, her damp lips softly parted. She knew in these circumstances, men and women usually protected themselves with nonchalance. Oddly, she discovered she had no more desire for pretense than Zack did. "I feel it," she said on a wispy ribbon of breath.

A sudden smile swept over Zack's face. Damn, but he was happy. "Unbelievable. I gave up on feeling like this when I stopped believing in Santa Claus." And then he stood up, knowing far better than she did how close he was to losing control. The last thing he wanted to do was to erase that soft look of trust in her eyes. "Merry Christmas to me, and to you a good-night. Unfortunately, it's time for me to be a gentleman."

Anna gave him a shaky little smile, still sensitive to the bright and demanding feelings thick in the air between them. She knew he cared enough to leave when he wanted to stay. Surprise and tenderness ran through her like a bubbling fountain. "Good night, then."

His cue to leave. Slowly Zack walked backward out of the studio, holding her in his eyes as long as he possibly could. And when he reached the doorway, he dipped his head, draping his hand over his eyes with a gesture of mock weeping. "You have no idea how hard this is."

"I think I do," Anna said softly.

He looked up, peeking through his fingers. His grin grew; so did hers. His hand dropped and he stared at her for a few more seconds, warring with himself. He knew there was a very good reason to return to his room and behave himself. Unfortunately, it was difficult to remember what that reason was. His passion stayed with him like the whispered fragrance of her perfume, making his reluctant chivalry acutely painful.

"Do you think there's going to be an 'us'?" he asked suddenly, seizing on a topic that would keep him near her. "Since that first moment at the store in Providence when you literally fell into my arms, I can't stop wondering."

Neither can I, Anna thought. But she only said, "Nighty-night, Mr. Romantic Policeman."

"When you look at me like that..." Zack muttered, "all I want is to..."

"All you want is...?"

"Nothing. Never mind. I have to leave now, *fast.*"

And he did.

Restless and wide awake after Zack had left her, Anna wasn't able to sleep until nearly 4:00 a.m. She couldn't forget that she was alone in the house with him. He slept directly below her, so disturbingly near. Throughout the night her mind continually strayed to him, lingering on the memories of the past two days. She got barely three hours' sleep before the rosy light of a brand-new sunrise slanted through her bedroom window, nudging her back to awareness.

Fortunately, she had always been one who could get along with very little sleep. She showered and changed into beige shorts and a navy-blue baby T-shirt, leaving her wet hair loose to dry. Bright-eyed and eager to meet a new day, she went to the kitchen and fixed herself a typical "Anna"

breakfast: a can of cola and a whole lot of brown sugar
garnished sparingly with oatmeal. She hummed beneath her
breath as she popped her brown sugar/oatmeal in the micro-
wave.

Zack Daniels was here with her, in her world, in her life,
in her house. Her funny little smile belonged to him, to that
thought.

Looking out the kitchen window, she could see it was the
perfect weather to run barefoot through the cool, dewy
grass, and she fought against the urge to go upstairs and
wake him up to enjoy the sunrise. Still, Zack didn't know
her all that well, and she did have certain idiosyncrasies that
not everyone understood. Not too long ago her friend Frank
had dropped by for breakfast. Anna had made the mistake
of asking him to play Frisbee with her on the back lawn.
Frank had immediately gone into "distinguished judge
mode," looking at Anna as if she had a screw loose. Some
men had problems with letting their hair down.

Anna had a sneaking suspicion that Zack would enjoy a
good game of Frisbee, but it was not yet 7:00 a.m. and
they'd had a late night. She generously decided she would
allow him to sleep in a bit. When he woke up, she would
offer him her very last Pop-Tart, a generous gesture indeed.
Until she went into town and did some marketing, her op-
tions were somewhat limited. Besides, who didn't enjoy a
nice Pop-Tart?

Her plan had been to spend some quality time in the porch
swing, musing on her situation with Zack and Kyle, emphasis on Zack. Anna was beginning to wonder if she hadn't
taken a flying leap from the frying pan into the fire by bringing Zack home to discourage Kyle, yet she felt remarkably
happy. Something was indeed happening to her, and it felt
like something very good. She would enjoy her breakfast
while she relived last night's…*sigh*…kiss.

But as she headed out the front door, she could see that
the porch swing was already occupied.

Zack was seated with his bare feet propped up on the porch railing. He was wearing a pale-blue denim shirt hanging open over his jeans, looking like a rumpled Tom Sawyer. She was surprised at the surge of unexpected emotion that simply seeing him inspired, unable to control the goofy smile that had taken over her lips. Her curiosity about the man was running unchecked, and every moment she spent in his company piqued that curiosity even more. She doubted there was a woman in the world who could be kissed by him and not be permanently branded. He was like a candy bar, only bigger, longer-lasting and addictive. A lovely, luscious, industrial-size Snickers bar.

"It's about time," Zack commented, not taking his eyes off the rosy sunrise. "What a lazy girl you are, sleeping this late. I've been waiting for you to come out and play with me."

Anna laughed when she realized he was actually serious. "How long have you been waiting for me?"

"All my life," Zack replied immediately, breaking into a cherubic smile that put the sunrise to shame. Finally he allowed himself to look at her, something he had been wanting to do all night. Her hair was damp, spreading clingy wet patches on her thin T-shirt. Her bare, bronzed legs were long, toned and well-suited to a Coppertone commercial. He ate her with his famished eyes. She was blue-eyed ambrosia.

Sweet Anna was bewitching, a woman whose natural beauty was only complemented by morning light. Just as he had suspected. She deserved a treat, he thought, for being wonderful. He pulled a candy necklace out of his front jeans pocket, the last souvenir of their memorable stay at Appleton's. "In the past couple of days, I kind of noticed you have a thing for sugar, so I brought this along for you."

Anna grinned, licking the sugar off the back of her spoon. "Thank you. I'll save it for dessert. I'm impressed—Mr. Romantic Policeman is also thoughtful and unselfish."

"You forgot good-looking," Zack remarked sadly, knowing very well he wasn't exactly a picture of beauty with his unshaven face. He'd managed to shower, but he'd been too anxious to see Anna again to take time to shave.

"Oh, good-looking goes without saying. And since you were so nice to bring me a treat, I'll share my oatmeal with you."

"You're a wonderful hostess, and I'm very glad you're *finally* awake. So…wanna play a game?"

"That depends on the game." Smiling, she nestled in the swing beside him, tucking one bare leg beneath her. It felt good, like they'd been sharing a porch swing for years. "I've never met anyone who loved to play like you do."

"You sound like Captain Todd. He says everyone else on the force is an adult, but I'm merely in disguise. Can you believe it?"

Her smile grew to a grin. "Maybe he's just jealous of how much you enjoy your life."

"I love the way you think. You see, life is a very short walk from the cradle to the grave, and I've always believed you should pack in as much quality time in between as possible. It's all in your attitude." Zack basked in her incredible smile, wondering if he would ever become immune to it. To distract him from those kissable lips, he reverted to one of his favorite childhood pursuits. "I noticed you have a lot of clover in your lawn. There's bound to be some magic in there somewhere."

She stared at him, her spoon frozen in midair. Last night had left her with a very erotic interpretation of magic. "What do you mean?"

He read her mind, grinning. "Four-leaf clovers, *duh*. They're a cop's best friend, next to his gun. Finish up your oatmeal, Anna. We're going hunting for some luck."

The morning was warm, the air gentle with sea breeze and floating wisps of apple blossoms. Thinking back, Anna couldn't remember ever playing games as a child. She had grown up much too quickly, and there were always things to worry about besides entertainment. Oddly, since meeting Zack, her whole life felt like a wonderful game. The satisfaction didn't come from playing chess or Candyland or hunting for lucky four-leaf clovers, but from simply being in his company. Zack had a confident, contagious masculine charm that somehow transformed mundane, everyday living into a grand adventure. He never seemed to be bored, and heaven knew he was never boring. From Appleton's to McDonald's to the little town of Grayland Beach, Zack Daniels lived life double-time, and he'd been kind enough to take Anna along for the ride.

Fortunately, she'd finally learned what is was to have been unconditionally loved by her adoptive parents, but her supposedly "carefree" childhood days had been long gone by then. At the ripe old age of twenty-six, it felt wonderful to relax and try her hand at being a child. Still, when Anna looked into Zack's eyes and saw the sensual awareness teasing her there, she remembered that not everything between them was innocent.

Anna had no sense of time passing until a familiar four-door sedan pulled up in front of her house, distracting her from carving her initials with Zack's handy-dandy Swiss Army knife in the bark of her apple tree. She let out a little whimper, watching Carrie get out of the driver's seat and Kyle climb out from the passenger side. Davy and Frank scrambled out from the rear seat. It was too early for a confrontation, but it seemed she had no choice. Kyle had apparently rallied the troops.

"Good Lord," Zack said with horror, his resentful gaze sticking immediately on Kyle. "It's like one of those clown cars where they never stop climbing out. You have way too many friends, kiddo."

"Try to behave yourself," Anna whispered out the side of her mouth, at the same time reaching out to hug Carrie. "Hey! Long time no see."

"I can't believe you're back!" Carrie replied, returning

the hug. "I was so happy when Kyle told me you had come back early. Did you have a good time in San Francisco?" Her smiling brown eyes slid to Zack. "My, oh, my. It certainly *looks* like you had a good time."

"I did?" Anna asked blankly. Then, when Zack nudged her by stepping on her toes, "*Ouch*. Oh, yes. Yes, I...well, I met Zack there, and you know how it goes. Things happen. Plans change."

Carrie smiled at Zack, sticking out her hand. "I owe you big-time if you're the reason Anna came back early enough to help me with the wedding. I'm Carrie Wagner."

"Zack Daniels." Zack dispensed with the handshake, giving Carrie a brief hug instead. She was nearly as tall as he was, with short, flyaway butterscotch hair and soft Bambi eyes. She also sported a healthy dusting of freckles on her sun-kissed cheeks, which Zack thought were adorable. But best of all she was the reason he'd been invited to come to Grayland Beach in the first place. "I like you already. We're going to be friends."

At that moment Kyle got in his face, blocking Zack's view of his new friend Carrie and irritating him greatly. "The veterinarian is back," he said flatly. "Whoopee."

"I told my friends all about you, Zack," Kyle replied. "They really wanted to meet you."

Judging by the suspicious looks on the surrounding faces, Zack figured he'd been painted as some kind of serial killer. "It's awfully early in the morning for a lynching. I'm flattered you were all so anxious. You know, Kyle, you didn't tell me last night how adorable your fiancée was."

Kyle had the grace to flush. "We didn't have much time to talk last night. But you're right, Carrie *is* wonderful."

"You're a lucky man," Zack went on, delivering an unmistakable message with his hard gray eyes. "Why is it we don't always appreciate our blessings, I wonder?"

"Too early in the morning for deep thoughts," Anna interrupted quickly, stepping between them. She felt like a defenseless little kitty-cat between two snarling pit bulls. She grabbed for Davy's hand and tugged him into the little group. "Zack, you haven't met everyone. This is Davy. I told you about him—he's a cover model for romance novels. Very much in demand, by the way. The ladies love him, especially when his shirt is off."

"Please," Davy muttered. "Don't *do* that to me. I was curious to meet you, Daniels. I've known Anna since I was in high school. Her late father was my football coach. I was a lineman." Then, with an unmistakable note of challenge in his voice: "Protection, that's what I learned from Carson Smith. Guard your quarterback, that's always been my motto."

"Frank," Anna called desperately, depending on her old friend's good manners and maturity to smooth over the ruffled feathers. "I need you."

A gray-haired fellow in a spotless peach-colored golf shirt and perfectly creased slacks stepped forward, shaking Zack's hand. "I'm certain Anna has spoken about me," he said in a perfectly clipped, radio announcer's deep voice. "My name is—"

"No, no, wait," Zack said, grinning widely. "You've got to be the lawyer."

"I am a *judge,"* he intoned, reminding Zack forcibly of Charlton Heston playing Moses in *The Ten Commandments.* "Judge Franklin Archibald Carstairs."

"But you were a lawyer before you were a judge," Zack replied innocently, "right? I have this thing about lawyers. I can spot them a mile away. So, does anyone here want to check me for clean underwear or inspect my teeth? I don't mind, really. You can investigate me from top to bottom. That's what they did before I was accepted into the police academy, and I passed with flying colors. I can even have my credit report sent up if you'd like."

Davy glared at Kyle as if to say, *He's not the spawn of Satan you told us he was.* "You got me up at eight o'clock on a Saturday morning for this? To meet a *policeman* you think is untrustworthy?''

"I've died and gone to hell," Anna said sadly. Her cheeks were blazing, and she couldn't bring herself to look in Carrie's eyes. Carrie was no fool. Her fiancé's concern for Anna was awfully personal for a man who was supposed to be nothing more than a friend. "One of these days you'll all have to accept the fact that I'm all grown-up."

"I doubt it," Frank said, oh-so-carefully picking a spot of lint off his slacks. "You'll always be cute little Anna Smith to us. Kyle, I believe you overreacted. Zack seems normal. Not at all the slimy, opportunistic gigolo you painted him as." Then, with an inquiring glance at Zack, "You don't have any tattoos, do you?"

Zack blinked. "Tattoos? No."

"Well, there you have it," Frank said to Kyle. "You said he was covered with tattoos."

Kyle cleared his throat. "I thought I saw tattoos."

"You know," Frank continued, obviously intent on doing his duty, "one of these days you and I are going to have a serious talk about the legal repercussions of slander and discrimination."

"I'm covered with *tattoos?*" Zack chortled, raising his eyebrows at Kyle. "Oh, that's a good one. Kyle, one of these days you and I are going to have a serious talk, too, all about the serious repercussions of annoying me. And as far as the rest of you are concerned, I'm a cop, not a slimy, opportunistic gigolo. And I wouldn't hurt Anna for the world."

And to prove his point, he kissed her.

It wasn't a passionate maneuver, to say the least. Zack pulled Anna to him gently by her wrist, his merry eyes dancing as he pressed a smile briefly against her lips. Despite the casual manner of the caress, despite the fact it was strictly for show and had a built-in audience, Anna felt the resulting electricity ripple through her veins like liquid fire.

It had been, she thought with sudden clarity, roughly nine hours since he had kissed her last. She hadn't realized until now that she was counting.

Frank cleared his throat tactfully, staring with great fascination at the rain gutter running along the eaves of the house. Davy stuffed his hands in his pockets and scuffed at a dandelion with his sneaker. But Kyle was staring at Anna and Zack, his jaw set in stone and his gaze dark and flat. He didn't notice that his fiancée was taking in his odd reaction, her smile drifting away.

Post kiss, it took Anna two tries before she was able to speak with her normal voice. "Well, since you're all here, you may as well come in for breakfast. It's Saturday, so I suppose no one has to worry about going in to work?"

"Actually," Carrie said quietly, "I have some things to do this morning. I need to be on my way. If the rest of you want to stay—"

"No, we'll leave with you." Kyle abruptly turned and marched back to the car without another word. Carrie's soft brown eyes followed him, her expression briefly uncovered to reveal a stark pain. "I guess...he has wedding nerves. He's been a bachelor for much too long, I'm afraid. Sorry for barging in on you like this, Anna."

"It's good to see you again," Anna told her quietly. "You and I should go out to dinner before the wedding. Girls' night out."

"That would be great," Carrie said in a hollow voice. "Zack, I hope you'll excuse my fiancé. He's actually a nice guy when he isn't about to be married."

"I'm sure he is," Zack said gently. He bent down and kissed Carrie lightly on the cheek. Then he looked at Kyle who was standing beside the car, noting the little kiss had attracted the man's full attention. Good. Dr. Doolittle needed a wake-up call, and Zack Daniels was just the man to give it to him. He gave Kyle a sunny smile, waving cheerfully. "See ya, Kyle. Don't be a stranger, good buddy."

Six

You could tell a lot about a man at the produce section in the market.

Zack seemed to enjoy the experience of shopping for food as he enjoyed everything else he did in his life. Little or big, he took everyday, mundane occurrences and made them into original, enjoyable experiences.

"You're not supposed to juggle apples in the store," Anna told him firmly.

"You should take a risk now and then. It's very exhilarating."

"There are people staring at—"

"I don't see them," Zack said. "And I certainly don't let them distract me from entertaining myself. Now I'm going to teach you how to juggle."

Anna ended up buying thirteen very bruised apples in the wake of her juggling lesson. The rest of their purchases were heavy on calories, cholesterol and preservatives and light on nutrition. They also bought a couple of frozen pizzas at

PLAY THE
Lucky Key Game

and you can get

FREE BOOKS
and a FREE GIFT!

Do You Have the LUCKY KEY?

Scratch the gold areas with a coin. Then check below to see the books and gift you can get!

YES!
I have scratched off the gold areas. Please send me the 2 FREE BOOKS and GIFT for which I qualify. I understand I am under no obligation to purchase any books, as explained on the back of this card.

326 SDL DNVG   225 SDL DNVC

FIRST NAME   LAST NAME

ADDRESS

APT.#   CITY

STATE/PROV.   ZIP/POSTAL CODE

2 free books plus a free gift   1 free book

2 free books   Try Again!

Visit us online at
www.eHarlequin.com

BUSINESS REPLY MAIL
FIRST-CLASS MAIL   PERMIT NO. 717-003   BUFFALO, NY

POSTAGE WILL BE PAID BY ADDRESSEE

SILHOUETTE READER SERVICE
3010 WALDEN AVE
PO BOX 1867
BUFFALO NY 14240-9952

NO POSTAGE
NECESSARY
IF MAILED
IN THE
UNITED STATES

Zack's request. Cops loved pizza, he told Anna. That, and a whole lot of coffee. They had a reputation for eating only donuts, but although donuts had their revered place in a cop's life, a little variety was necessary.

Anna tried to reconcile the Zack she knew with the Zack who dealt with the darker side of humanity each and every day. She'd had a taste of that as a child, enough to give her some idea of what he faced in the course of his work. He'd seen the worst of people in the worst of circumstances, yet nothing seemed to have dulled his appetite for life with all its infinite adventures. She watched him as they strolled out to the parking lot, his black hair beating softly in the wind, powerful shoulders stretching the soft fabric of his pale-blue shirt, narrow hips rolling with a lazy, catlike grace. The sun caught the smoothness of his skin and the hard curve of his jaw, polishing his dark California tan. And his smile, that teasing, "anything goes" smile was perpetually rearranging the pattern of Anna's heartbeat. Even carrying two bags of groceries, the man did *not* look domestic. Rather, he looked like something out of a wonderful dream she might have had, a fantasy too bright, too charming, too perfect to exist amongst the ordinary realities of life.

He looked like a hero. And for the moment, *her* hero.

The stronger her attraction to him, the more she reminded herself to keep an eye on her heart. There was a huge gap between Anna Smith and Zack Daniels. She was a woman who couldn't wait to go home at night. He was a man who couldn't bear to tear himself away from work. She adored her security, he craved a challenge. The very things Anna had escaped from so long ago Zack willingly dealt with day after day. For the moment he could visit her world, but she knew without a doubt he could never thrive in it.

It was a good thing for her to remember.

"We could have done this in my car," Zack told her, setting the groceries in the back of the Jeep. "It has plenty of room behind the front seats."

"At least enough room for the tortilla shells," she replied wryly. "Besides, it probably takes more gasoline to start that nuclear-powered engine than it does for my car to drive to the east coast and back. It can't be economical."

Zack cleared his throat, avoiding her eyes. "Are you big on economy?"

"I'm big on reality. When you're a kindergarten teacher for Head Start, you have to accept an unimpressive salary in exchange for personal satisfaction. I don't really mind. I get along fine if I'm careful. But it's second nature to count pennies." A pause, then curiously, "Isn't it the same for you? Cops are right up there with teachers on the underpaid scale, aren't they? Especially when you consider you're out there risking your life every day."

Zack didn't want to risk their newfound closeness by telling her it would be damn near impossible to count all the pennies he had. Neither did he want to lie to her. He decided to change the subject.

He grinned, spinning neatly on his heel and deftly backing her against the driver's door. His legs trapped hers on either side, his hands resting on the rag top of the Jeep above her head. "Guess what? I can think of more entertaining things to do besides talk about my salary. Let's play a game."

"Of *course* you want to play a game. And just what kind—"

That was all she had time to say before his mouth swooped over hers. It was fast, hard and instantly heated. They kissed beneath a cloudless sky, Zack's mouth moving hungrily over hers like a starving man. The kiss uncovered so much so quickly—the passion and curiosity that had been building between them since the first moment they met. There were people around, cars pulling in and out of the parking lot, seagulls shrieking low in the air, but they all belonged to a different world. Anna and Zack pressed hard together in their own universe, her hands clinging to his shoulders with sudden, fierce strength. His mouth tasted like sunshine, bright and warm and fresh as summer dew. Anna hadn't realized how very much she was craving his touch again.

Graphic and uncontrolled, the wanting spilled inside of her like a shower of white-hot sparks. The sun poured down yellow and gold, hot on their hair, their skin. Anna gasped against his mouth as his hands pulled her against him, into the sweet cradle of his hips. She fitted against him so beautifully, as if he was the puzzle piece that had been missing from her life so long.

A horn honked in the parking lot, then another. Zack pulled away gently, his breathing coming in hard catches, his eyes dark and deep. "We're attracting attention. I don't know if I care."

Anna leaned weakly against the Jeep for balance. It was hard to come up with something intelligent to say when heartbeats were rippling into her throat and her mind was numb. The door he had opened for her back in Appleton's General Store would not close. "What *was* the name of this game, anyway?"

"Have you heard of the game called Sorry?"

"Yes..."

"Well, that wasn't it."

"I see." There was a shaky thread of laughter in her voice. Washed with sunlight, Zack was bold, charming and dramatic, with a lilting humor in his gray eyes. In some distant part of her mind, she knew she was falling deeper into a situation she wasn't capable of controlling or even understanding. She knew, and in that moment, she didn't care. The level of simple happiness she felt was intoxicating.

In a parking lot, of all places.

"I was just practicing for when we see Dr. Doolittle again," Zack explained meekly.

"I'm sure." She tried to scowl at him, but it was impossible. Instead she broke out in laughter and punched him lightly in the arm. "Come on, Mr. Romantic Policeman. We wouldn't want our ice-cream sandwiches to melt. Or the Popsicles, or the—"

"I get the point," Zack said. "We must discuss your priorities one day."

When they returned home, a surprise awaited.

Carrie had returned, her car parked at the curb in front of the house. She sat on the porch swing with her arms wrapped around her chest, a small suitcase at her feet.

"Oh-oh," Zack drawled. "Methinks we have a crisis."

"That damn Kyle," Anna muttered, shoving open the door. "What has he done now?"

Once inside the house, the three of them shared the sofa while Carrie made short work of her explanation. "I left him," she said flatly, dabbing at her swollen eyes with a tissue Anna had given her. "We had an argument and I left him. It wasn't until I'd walked out of his house that I realized I had nowhere to go. I gave up my apartment when I moved in with him last month. Anna, I'm so sorry to barge in on you like this, but I don't know where else to go."

"I'm glad you came here," Anna reassured her. "I'm happy you felt you could."

"It's such an imposition. I'm interrupting your time with Zack—"

"Not at all," Zack said cheerfully. "Believe me, you're not an imposition. Now, if *Kyle* had showed up here, that would have been another—"

"*Zack.*" Anna narrowed her eyes at him, effectively cutting short his tirade. Then she turned to Anna. "What was the argument about?"

"You," Carrie said in a small, forlorn voice.

Zack and Anna exchanged wide-eyed looks. "About me?" Anna squeaked. "What about me?"

"Anna, I'm not blind. I knew Kyle was getting really nervous about the wedding. He's gone so long being a footloose bachelor that he's seizing on any excuse to change his mind. Since his best friend also happens to be incredibly beautiful, he distracted himself with fantasies about you. After Zack kissed you today in front of us, Kyle went ballistic. I couldn't pretend it didn't matter. Not any longer.''

Anna colored hotly. "Carrie, I have never—''

"Oh, I know you've never thought of him as anything but a friend," Carrie said, waving her tissue dismissively in the air. "I'm not blaming you one bit. It's just that I thought he would get over this, but it's not happening. It hurts too much to put up with it, Anna. If the man is too stupid to realize what really matters to him, I'm gone.''

"I'm so sorry," Anna said miserably. "I don't know what else to say. Men are idiots.''

"Ahem," Zack said, feeling it necessary to remind them that not *all* men were idiots. "Let's stop criticizing men and just concentrate on criticizing Kyle, okay? You deserve better, Carrie. Maybe now you're gone, he'll figure out what his priorities are. Would you like me to go over to his house and beat him up?'' Then, when Anna's eyes shot daggers at him: "I was just trying to be helpful, *honey.*''

Carrie shrugged, blowing her nose loudly. "Nothing will help. It's over. You know, in a way I'm so glad you and Zack are together. It makes this a little easier, if such a thing is possible.''

"Well…good," Anna said lamely. Her guilt was doubling and redoubling. Now she was not only responsible for Carrie's heartbreak, albeit indirectly, but she was also lying to her. *Oh, what a tangled web we weave…*

"Anna, if I can just stay for a few days until I find an apartment—''

"Of course you can," Anna told her gently. "As long as you want.''

Carrie briefly hugged her friend, tears overflowing once again. "I miss him already. Love is a horrible thing. Horrible.''

Zack sighed heavily, shaking his head. "I knew he was a jerk the first time I saw him."

"He's not a jerk," Carrie sniffed. "I love him."

She was being, Zack thought with confusion, somewhat schizophrenic. How could a woman hate and love, both at the same time? "All right," he said helplessly. "Whatever you say."

Carrie managed to give Zack a watery smile. "I'm sorry. It's just…this is hard. I'm so mixed up. Anna, you and Zack won't even know I'm here. I'll take the bedroom farthest down the hall from yours. I leave pretty early in the morning, so you two can sleep in. When you get up, I'll be gone."

Silence. With an inward jolt, Anna realized she was trapped. Carrie expected her to be spending the nights with Zack. In her room. Together. She looked at Zack and Zack looked at her, shrugging helplessly. Still, he didn't look unhappy. On the contrary, his eyes had a brand-new, "Boy, oh boy," sparkle.

"Just don't worry about a thing, Carrie," Anna managed. "We'll love having you."

"Absolutely," Zack seconded. "And like you said, Carrie, *our* room is way down the other end of the hall from yours. We'll have all the privacy we want in *our* room. Isn't that right, Anna? *Our* room is pretty secluded."

Anna barely suppressed the urge to throw something at him. With teeth grinding, she said, "Whatever you say, Zack."

Zack beamed at Carrie. "See? This situation is going to have a harmonious outcome, I just know it."

Anna's home was beginning to feel like a bed-and-breakfast inn. As they were finishing their dinner that evening, there was a heavy pounding on the front door, combined with the simultaneous ringing of the doorbell.

"Kyle," Carrie said immediately, looking panicked. "I'd know that knock anywhere."

"Not to worry, ladies." Zack pushed his chair back from the table, a bright light of anticipation gleaming in his eyes. "I can handle this with no problem. I'm very experienced when it comes to domestic disturbances."

A few moments later Kyle trailed Zack into the kitchen.

"He won't go away," Zack explained, shrugging his broad shoulders. "Being on my best behavior, as I promised, I thought I'd better ask Carrie before I throw him out. Carrie? Can I throw him out, please?"

Kyle gave no sign of even hearing Zack's merry prattle. His complete attention was fixated on Carrie. "I want you to come home, Carrie," he said quietly. "We can't talk here."

"I don't have a home," Carrie said, casually taking a sip of her water. "Tomorrow I'm looking for an apartment. Anna, this dinner is wonderful. You'll have to give me the recipe for the salad."

"Oh, for Pete's sake." Kyle glanced at Anna. "Tell her to listen to me. Help me out here."

"This situation is your fault," Anna replied coolly, forking a bit of lettuce. "It's between you and Carrie."

"I'm having the best time," Zack put in happily. "There's always so much going on here in Grayland Beach. This is a very entertaining place, every bit as fun as Los Angeles."

"We need to talk, Carrie," Kyle persisted stubbornly, a muscle ticking in his jaw. "You're overreacting."

For a moment, Carrie only stared at him. Then she went back to her food. "I didn't overreact. I took off my blinders. Go away, Kyle."

"What she said," Zack put in.

"I haven't done anything *wrong*," Kyle said.

"You're breathing," Zack murmured, staring angelically at the ceiling as he rocked back and forth on his heels.

Kyle turned on him. "One more crack out of you—"

"Enough already!" Anna stood up, taking a fistful of Zack's shirt and planting him firmly in his chair. "Kyle, it's time for you to leave. Carrie isn't ready to talk to you."

"Why the hell aren't you helping?" Kyle demanded. "Don't you know what's happening here? Everything has gone to hell! Why doesn't anyone care about it but *me?*"

"Possibly," Anna said tightly, "because it's all your fault. Go home and think about that, Kyle. You have no right to be angry. None at all."

"None at all," Carrie echoed, lowering her lids so Kyle couldn't see the tears misting in her eyes.

What was once a delicate situation had become a monumental snarl.

Like warriors facing off, Anna stood on one side of her bed and Zack on the other. They had just bidden Carrie good-night, then walked hand in hand down the hall to Anna's room. "This is just for show," Anna had whispered out of the side of her mouth. "It's not real."

"Of course," Zack had replied angelically. Lately it seemed that his fairy godmother was working overtime, and he was most grateful. "Not to worry, sweet pea."

Anna was now facing the fallout from her brilliant charade. There was one bed and two people. In this particular situation, two into one did not go.

No wonder "Thou shalt not lie" was one of the ten commandments. Lying got a person in terrible trouble.

"Don't look like that," Anna warned Zack. "Don't you *dare.*"

"Look like what?"

"Like you're enjoying all this."

"I *am* enjoying all this," Zack said defensively. Then he took a good look at her and decided to ease up. Poor Anna had that same look of panic she'd had just before she'd passed out on him in Appleton's. "Anna, you've got to know by now that you can trust me. I would never take advantage of a situation like this." Honesty compelled him to add: "I would *want* to, naturally. But I would manfully resist."

Anna's mind was going in ten directions at once. She wasn't woman enough to admit that she, too, had thought about the intimate possibilities of their new sleeping arrangement. He might take that as an invitation, and she might not discourage him quite as fervently as she should...if at all. She knew she was intensely susceptible to his dark good looks and wayward charm. No woman with a pulse could be immune to him.

And here they were, standing with a bed between them and a long night to pass.

"I think I know how to deal with this," Zack offered gently, when Anna went a full sixty seconds without so much as blinking. "You're looking a little apprehensive, Anna. Like a little lamb who finds herself forced to share a bed with the big, bad wolf."

"That's absurd," she muttered. But *true*.

"You're worried I'll try something?"

"Not at all." *Of course.*

"Then what if I kiss you good-night and get it over with? That will kind of defuse the situation, take the 'what if' out of it. Then we sleep. I'll sleep with all my clothes on. I'd advise you to wear something, too, but that's completely up to you."

Anna chewed on her fingernail, studying him. His suggestion was ridiculous, but in a strange way it made sense. If they went ahead and took the guesswork out of the situation, the sensual tension just might dissipate. Just one kiss, then a good night's sleep. In the morning, all her fears would have proven unfounded. They would be friends, pals, buddies again.

Ha.

"I'd never hurt you," Zack told her quietly. He couldn't

think of a single reason why she should take his word for this, but hoped she would. For whatever reason, his physical needs came in second to her emotional needs. "What can I do to convince you of that?"

"You can still be my friend in the morning," she whispered. "*Just* my friend. More than anything else, that's what I want right now. I'm not ready for anything else, Zack. Part of me wishes I was, but I don't think I am."

His eyes darkened with something that was almost pain. "If that's what you want from me, Anna, that's what I'll give you. Friendship."

If she was honest with herself, Anna knew there was more she wanted from Zack. But not yet. Not tonight, when they were alone in her bedroom only because of accidental circumstances and one whopping lie.

"My hero," she managed, an uncertain smile flirting with her lips. "Kiss me good-night, then."

For an instant Zack was paralyzed. She trusted him. He desperately wanted to go beyond a simple kiss, so it wouldn't be easy. Having someone's trust put a whole new spin on things. It demanded something of him, something beyond his own desires.

It was a new feeling, but it wasn't a bad feeling.

Afterward, he didn't remember walking around the bed to her. He only knew that one moment he was far away, the next he was enfolding her in his arms with sweet gentleness. He couldn't pause to talk or even smile, or his concentration might be broken. He was tiptoeing across a tightrope of tenuous control. The touch of his lips on hers was as gentle as starlight, lingering almost imperceptibly before he pulled away. It was a chaste kiss, a friend's kiss. It was also a form of damned masochism.

"Thank you," Anna said softly, trying not to sound disappointed. *Be careful of what you want,* she thought, *because you just might get it.*

"I didn't do that right," Zack said sadly. "Just one more, and I promise not to mess this one up. Do you mind?"

His smile stretched at that; so did hers. It seemed the most natural thing in the world for Zack to pull her close again, his chest making a tantalizing, caressing weight on her breasts. His hips found hers, pushing with the faintest, unconscious yearning. Seeking against her mouth, his lips carefully urged hers into a heated openness, as if she were a prized, very rare delicacy he was tasting for the first time. His tongue touched inside her mouth, and he heard the sudden hiss of her indrawn breath. He thought nothing had ever felt so good in his entire life as this kiss.

He couldn't bring himself to pull away completely. Instead, he rested his forehead on hers, his lips parted on uneven breaths. His hands stroked her hair, again and again. Meanwhile, he chanted his own silent mantra: *I am not taking this further. I am not taking this further....*

Anna's throat was tight and burning. It was amazing, knowing how Zack's body yearning against hers could affect her. And, in a strange way, it was also frightening.

She knew what he was, who he was. Zack was just a fleeting moment in her life, someone who was just visiting her peaceful, predictable world. She craved permanence. He lived for the heat of the moment. Again, two polar opposites into one did not go. But how could she cope with the sizzling frenzy of need he'd kindled to life within her? She was no longer in this strange relationship up to her neck; she was in way, way, *way* over her head. Even if she gave in to her own pressing need for him, the outcome would still be the same. She would remain in Grayland Beach with her house and her friends and her snug little life. He would go off to his next adventure, heroically righting wrongs and fighting injustice along the way. And yet, some devil made her say softly, like a child asking for a treat, "One more kiss, Zack. Please."

She wasn't making this easy, Zack thought desperately,

stung by the midnight-blue passion in her eyes. And with his limited control where she was concerned, anything could happen if he let down his guard. He lowered his head, gently ruffling soft kisses along her cheek. He didn't mean to let it go further, but it seemed the road to hell—and possibly heaven—was paved with good intentions. His questing lips found hers again, his entire world narrowed to her silk-and-satin mouth. Caution turned to frantic, fierce hunger without asking permission. Her body felt so small, so delicate, and he could feel the warmth of her skin through the clothes she wore. He kissed, he drank deeply, then his seeking mouth danced in sweet disbelief over her face, her neck, her hair. His hand curled over the burgeoning curve of her breast, and discovered that her thundering pulse matched his own. He fed on her and she on him, desperately needy. He truly didn't know how long they stood fused together, how many kisses he gave or how many kisses she returned. It might have been a minute, ten minutes, longer. Her hips were pushing hard against his and her breath was coming in hard catches. Zack's blood was eighty-proof adrenaline, zinging through his veins. He knew he was in trouble, and trouble had never frightened him like it did now.

Her eyelids had drifted closed, but Zack forced his to open. Fortitude, he thought grimly. That's the ticket. Despite his show of false confidence, he didn't trust himself one iota, not when it came to this incredibly appealing woman. Lips still on hers, he focused fiercely on a miniature Victorian lamp next to the bed. Bulb, he thought, stained glass, pull chain, red fringe. These thoughts were meant to keep his mind off what he was doing, but it was a lot to expect from a little Victorian lamp. If just kissing her was this hard on his willpower, what would eight hours sleeping next to her on a mattress do to him?

And then his eyes closed again and his thought processes shut down. He was only a man, and it seemed some things were out of the realm of possibility. Before Zack knew what had happened, he was sitting on the bed with Anna. His heart literally jumped with the shock of having so little control. He stood up so rapidly that Anna fell backward on the bed with a little gasp.

"I'm sorry, I'm sorry, I'm sorry," Zack muttered, wishing there was a third person somewhere in the room to physically restrain him from going back to kissing her. Instead, he had to depend only on himself, and he didn't feel terribly dependable. "Anna, despite the way it looked, I didn't plan that. Tell me to go sleep in the closet and I will. Tell me to make a bed in the bathtub and I will. I promise not to touch you again."

Softly, with an earnest look from her big, sad eyes, "Ever?"

"Hell, *no*. This is only an eight-hour promise, kiddo." Then, catching the expression on her face, he sighed deeply. "You're teasing me. The kidder has been kidded."

"Yes," Anna admitted, grinning a little. "I was teasing you, Mr. Romantic Policeman. You see? I do trust you, Zack. This is tricky, but not impossible. I could hardly make jokes if I was worried about losing my virtue."

Mentally Zack did a double take. "What? Anna? What's that you said about your virtue?"

Anna sat up on the edge of the bed, hands propped behind to steady her shaky body. "I said I'm not worried about losing it in the dead of night. Are you all right?"

"Of course. No. I don't know. I was just...putting two and two together, so to speak. So, you've never...you are still..."

"A virgin," she supplied, pulling a face. "What can I say? I guess I'm terribly picky." Silence took over. It was very loud. Finally Anna stood up, looking uncertainly around the room. The magic had disappeared, and acute self-consciousness had taken over. "Well...I guess we should get some sleep. You don't need to worry about going in the closet, Zack. I do trust you. Strangely, right now it's myself I don't trust.''

"What are you afraid of?" he asked softly, his hand touching her arm.

"That's a good question." She deliberately avoided his eyes, looking down at the floor. "I suppose…I know what's good for me and I know what's risky. I always have. The thing that scares me is that I'm starting not to care."

"I'm not such a bad guy," he replied quietly. "Maybe you should give me a chance to prove it."

She smiled faintly. "I know you're not a bad guy, Zack. It's me. I've always known what I needed to be happy. I'm an old-fashioned girl. I like predictability and security. But you…you're like a summer storm. They're absolutely amazing up here on the coast. Fast, unexpected, mesmerizing…and then gone as quickly as they came. You aren't good for me that way. What's more, I think you know it as well as I do."

And what could he say to that? Zack understood her completely. He knew what he was, and he knew what he wasn't. But oh, how he wanted her. How very much he wanted to tell her that she was wrong, that she *could* depend on him. Unfortunately, nothing in his life had ever convinced him that he was a man that a woman could depend on in the long run.

In his mind's eye, he saw his father. He remembered his bravado and his hollow, quick promises, and he remembered how his mother had withered a little more each time those promises were broken. Zack had always known he had something of his father in him. Fortunately, he had tried to learn from his father's mistakes. He wouldn't offer anyone more than he was capable of giving.

He turned away from her, his thoughts burning him. His emotions were no longer segregated in an orderly, comfortable way. He needed her with his body and he needed her with his soul. In those circumstances, acting on that need would be the most selfish thing he could do.

"I'm going downstairs to get a drink," he muttered. When the going got tough, the tough had a few stiff drinks before their desires got the better of them. "I'll be back in a while."

"Zack—"

"*No.*" He couldn't take the chance of looking at her and losing his resolve. "Don't say anything more, Anna. Just let me go."

Seven

Just let me go.

Anna heard those words echoing in her mind throughout the endless, aching night. She slept intermittently, waking in the early hours of the morning to discover Zack sleeping precariously on the far edge of the mattress, not only fully clothed but also on top of the bedspread. The man was taking no chances when it came to keeping his word. For the first time since her parents had died, Anna felt cherished. Her heart twisted in all directions as a strange acceptance settled gently in her heart. Something was happening in her…or perhaps it had happened some time ago, and she was just understanding it now.

She slipped out of bed and pulled a blanket from the linen closet in the hall, spreading it over him. She couldn't see his face in the darkness, but his breathing was irregular, as if his dreams were something less than pleasant. For some strange reason, she, too, chose to stretch out on top of the covers when she got back in bed, pulling the blanket over her, as well. Though she didn't touch him, she stayed close enough to feel the warmth of his body next to hers.

Anna hadn't slept in a bed with anyone since leaving her last group home in what seemed like a million years before. Back then, she had usually shared a bed with another girl, as space was always at a premium. The arrangements were never permanent. There were always new places to live— she never thought of them as homes—and new people to get used to. It made Anna very cautious of letting anyone too close too soon.

With her male friends, those men who had known and loved her father, it was different. She knew that whatever happened, they would always be there for her. But loving and being in love were two very different things. Until she was secure enough to take a risk, wagering her emotions had always seemed to be a tricky and precarious business.

And it still was. But suddenly, with Zack, it felt worth the risk.

Anna curled up on her side, watching him sleep for the longest time. Her thoughts were deep and wistful, a woman's battle between her head and heart. She knew the night hours were dwindling down to a precious few. When the sun rose, this odd stillness, this period of introspection would be lost. Would she ever be able to watch him sleeping again? Nothing was permanent—she'd learned that lesson at an early age. Whether she smiled and loved, or pounded her fists and shed tears of frustration, this night would soon pass into yesterday. Not forgotten, perhaps, but gone.

She became aware of frosty tentacles of fear clutching like a fist in her stomach. Without consciously making the decision, she closed her mind to everything but Zack. Very deliberately, she reached out a hand, resting it gently on his chest. He must have been sleeping lightly, for his eyes flew open immediately.

He turned his head toward her, asking a sleepy question with his eyes. Looking at her face, he realized he already knew the answer. There were no wounds in her shadowed expression, only a soft peace that sent his resolve scurrying in all directions. Panic set in, chattering at him. "Anna—"

"Shhh," she whispered, placing two fingers over his lips. "No talking, Zack."

A new light fired in his eyes as they held hers. He kissed the fingers on his lips, then he turned her hand over and kissed the sensitive skin of her palm. His muscles felt tight with the strain of wanting her. He no longer cared whether this was right or wrong. It was vital to him, just as vital as water and oxygen. It may have been his sleep-dulled mind, or the whiskey he'd had before coming back upstairs, but he was floating in a cloud of desire. He didn't want to think, not right now. He wanted to feel.

His expression was oddly tense as he stared at her. She was wearing some sort of pajama thing that looked like thermal underwear, and her hair was spread out over the pillow, clinging to her neck and curving around her face like a lovely velvet frame. She could cover herself with sackcloth and ashes, and it wouldn't dull her beauty. Or his need.

Again he asked the question with his glittering eyes. Again she gave him her answer, smiling ever so faintly. The desire that gave Zack no peace remained with him, a pitiless yearning. His pulse had become fast and hard, like steady running water. What had ever made him think he had control over this? Making love to Anna was inevitable, and had been since the first moment he saw her. Needing some sort of reassurance from someone wiser than himself, he looked above her head, staring out the window at the brilliant diadem of age-old stars. He felt like he had never really seen them before. Someone had control of this strange, sometimes hostile world, someone kind enough to light the darkness with the moon and the stars. In the past Zack hadn't often looked up at the night sky, usually because he was always busy watching his back. How strange that he could have gone so long without looking at the stars. He'd always been so concerned with the bad things in life that he'd missed much of the good. It was the nature of his work, and his work had been his life.

He turned on his side, face-to-face with Anna. He fell into her eyes, stunned at the wealth of emotion there. He felt himself slide right past his breaking point without even pausing, and found it hard to care. By bowing to her own need, Anna had freed him from his conscience. Wise or foolish, they had both made their choices.

His eyes skimmed her face, her hair, her lips. He lifted his hand almost as if in a trance, smoothing her hair, startled at the cool softness. How could anything in this room be cool when he was burning alive?

Her eyes shone like sapphires in her shadowed face. Zack searched them, but could see no sign of regret or uncertainty. He felt like a green schoolboy who had just been granted one wish. Shaking a little, he rose up on one elbow and kissed her softly on her forehead. His lips stayed close, his heart pounding, his breath tickling her skin. He felt her chest rise and fall with a shaky sigh. Looking down in her face, he found her watching him with a dizzying, drunk-on-love gaze. Holding her eyes, he kissed her gently on her rosebud lips. The kiss was tame for a moment, then immediately heated into a frenzy. He kissed her again and again, hands searching, mouth tasting, all the while wanting more and more and more. His need escalated almost instantly; he could hardly keep pace with it. His hands were on her face, holding her for his hungry mouth.

Anna was gasping, but there was no air in the room. She was light-headed, and way down in her belly she felt something twist, tighten and burn, all at once. Her anxious hands pushed back the material of his wrinkled, untucked shirt, yearning for smooth skin. She learned the curves of his chest, the flat ridges and rock-hard planes. She had never been hungry for a man before tonight. Her mind didn't know what it was to physically ache for someone. Her body had never felt empty before, or so anxious to be filled.

Until now. Until Zack, with his silver, restless eyes and sweet, wayward smile. How had she gone so long without this?

She was squirming on the bed, kicking impatiently at the covers. She had too many layers covering her, and that included her ugly-as-sin pajamas. Whatever had made her think that covering her body would cover her desire? Some things could never be changed, stifled or ignored. She wasn't in control of everything and probably never could be. Learning this lesson was somehow a relief.

Zack's heart was out of control. It had never been like this before, never. Moonlight gleamed over her hair, giving her an ethereal glow. Her rose-petal lips were dewed and swollen, parted on every gasping breath she took. She returned his stare fearlessly, and he saw something in her expression he hadn't noticed before: a gentle benediction. She had dedicated herself to him like an apostle, offering herself freely and willingly. There would be no turning back.

"Anna—"

"Don't." Again she shushed him with a shaky smile. She didn't want words right now. They got in the way. She looped her arms around his neck, pulling his head down to her chest and holding him tightly. Her breasts felt heavily weighted, aching to be touched. She wanted him everywhere, all over her body, within her body. Her hips began to move restlessly on the mattress. Nature was having her way with Anna, and she was relishing each and every second.

As if reading her mind, Zack's hungry hands pushed up the loose top of her pajamas, his palms finding the warm fullness of her breasts. Her nipples were as hard as pebbles, her heart was jumping frantically beneath her delicate skin. His mouth followed his hands, caressing her body with his lips and tongue. He suckled, he traced hot circles with his tongue. His hands slipped to her waist, but there he found the damned pajamas again. With short work, he had them off, tossing first the bottoms, then the top, over his shoulder and against the far wall. Needing became painful. His own clothes were stifling him, hot and heavy and frustrating.

He left her for a moment, making Anna smile with the way he took off his shirt, pulling it by the neck over his head without any thought given to make it look sexy. He emerged with his hair tumbled every which way and his smile self-consciously crooked. He shucked off his jeans, color staining his cheeks. Where had all his old confidence gone, all the smooth moves that had come so naturally to him? All the experience in the world couldn't have prepared him for this night with Anna.

She groaned with shocked pleasure when he came back to her, skin against skin. Never before in her life had she abandoned thought like this. There had been times when she had come close, but her fear of surrendering control had always kept her physical and emotional walls firmly between herself and the rest of the world. Tonight there were no walls; her long-suppressed wildness surprised her as much as it did Zack. Her enormous eyes were sweet and hot with passion.

He stared down at her face, his jaw clenched with a stabbing hunger. His wanting was crossing from pleasure to pain. It had never happened to him so quickly before, or so intensely. It had all been a game, and games offered only a brief enjoyment. Loving Anna was no game.

He could have stared at her forever, but if he *only* stared, it would kill him soon. Everything she was, everything he saw in her, begged to be possessed. His gaze moved hungrily over her face, her mouth, her body. Her shadowed cleavage tempted him with a siren's call, her flawless skin gleaming with hot, golden moisture. He loved her with his hands and with his lips, everywhere. In turn, she gave him a blizzard of tiny, nerve-shuddering openmouthed kisses, everywhere she could reach.

Anna's hands explored him, wanting to learn. She knew she could only learn to love by loving. All through her adult life she had thought that when she was ready for love, love would find her. And she had been right.

Zack went down to her in a hot, fluid movement, holding her face fiercely for an endless kiss. His body molded itself to hers, breast to breast, thigh to thigh. When he pulled back briefly, it was to stare at the beautiful creation of his desire. Her lovely, amazing eyes were dark blue with passion. Her mouth was parted and open, her hands holding tightly to his shoulders. Zack had no idea what he had ever done to merit her commitment to the moment. The intensity in her expression humbled him beyond words.

He stilled, closing his eyes for a moment. Then he lowered his head ever so slowly, kissing her forehead as one would kiss a child. The touch of his lips lingered on hers after the kiss was broken, brushing back and forth across her satin mouth. He learned the curves, the fullness, the shape and texture. His tongue lightly traced those sweet, perfect curves with tantalizing lightness. He was memorizing them, though he knew they would stay with him always, lingering in his memory like a brand on his soul. Their breath mingled into one body, one heart.

"Now?" Anna asked softly, the little word taking his world by storm.

Zack finally understood what it was to love *with* love. The completeness a certain woman, the right woman, brought to a man was almost more than he could grasp. Love and sex had always been two different things for him, one seemingly forever out of reach and the other so easy to attain he had doubted its value.

Oh, but loving with his heart as well as his body was a revelation. It was a tender warmth that curled in his loins and stretched into his mind and soul with pervasive gentleness. Zack realized with a strange shock that tonight was his first time, as well.

Anna loved the intensity in his eyes. It was amazing to her, the things he seemed to see in her. She had wondered what it would be like to love him almost from the first moment they met, but the reality was something else altogether. Her eyes drifted half-closed when his hands spanned her waist, her chin raising and pressing her head back in the pillow. She knew all she needed to know now, knew that this was as important to her as it was to him. This was the final wall that had stood between them, her fear of allowing a man to become necessary to her. Somehow, without Zack saying a word, she knew that she was safe with him.

Nature had ways of bringing a man and a woman together, and Anna instinctively knew her part. Her hips made a cradle for his, her shoulders straining up and off the mattress. Her nails were pressing into the skin of his back like tiny kitten claws. There was pain and there was pleasure, and there were needy hollows aching to be filled to overflowing. She was racked with hard shivers, cool goose bumps spreading over her warm flesh. For Anna, the only sounds in the room were Zack's hard breathing and her own heart thundering in her ears.

She lifted her hips in mute invitation, at the same time twisting languorously against the tumbled sheets. He nudged her legs farther apart, kissing her almost roughly. What little control he had before was now gone completely. A long strand of soft, tawny hair got tangled up between their lips and he flicked it aside impatiently. She gave back his kisses with equal urgency. But kisses would no longer suffice, and they both knew it.

Gasping, Zack held back the hair at the sides of her face with white-knuckled hands. His gaze locked hard with hers. Her legs widened, parting for him. When he hesitated, she lifted herself toward him, so hungry she felt she was going quietly out of her mind. There had to be something, a cure for her need. His head dropped back, lolling on his neck while he forcibly restrained himself. He released control in cautious measure, initiating her gradually until she was hot and fluid and lissome with readiness. He shook, and his breathing grew loud and ragged. There was no more control to be found.

His possession was slow and sacred, an endearment in itself. Her hands were tight around him, absorbing the barely leashed power in his straining muscles while she drew him in deeper. Zack passed on wonderful knowledge with the sinuous motions of his hips, muscles bunching in his arms on either side of her writhing body. And still, there were no words: they communicated through gasps and murmurs and heavy-eyed looks of need. Anna learned how much patience Zack was capable of, and Zack discovered that a woman's innocence was a fierce and overwhelming aphrodisiac.

There came a moment when their bodies strained and paused in the silent euphoria, both wanting to prolong the anticipation of release as long as humanly possible. Still, nothing could last forever, no matter how hard they wanted to hold on to it. Zack groaned and began moving again, matching her instinctive movements thrust for thrust, sword to sheath. They climbed higher, which neither of them had thought possible. Anna was fascinated, then quickly frantic. She felt the cool tracks of tears on her cheeks while her body wept with another sort of release. It was a union of bodies and minds, a beautiful poem and an endless mystery. And with all her imagining, she had never imagined anything as hallowed and renewing as this.

Moved deeply, Anna discovered that once was not enough for a twenty-six-year-old woman who had waited a lifetime for love. Finally she was where she belonged. And in turn, she showed Zack that twice was easily possible for a man, as well...given a bit of incentive from a novice with tremendous aptitude.

Then came another revelation. Afterward, the sweet, seeping pleasure gathered and pooled in the heavy shadows of the bedroom. Spent, exhausted and floating, they lay weakly in each other's arms while the world waited for them to return. Anna thought the moment was a miracle in itself, a little stretch of time while their bodies tangled together and rested. Her eyes were enormous, staring up at the ceiling in mute wonderment.

So this was heaven, the place beyond the little death of making love.

Afterward, she was hungry.

It was a swift drop back to earth from heaven, but one had to fortify one's strength. And so, at five in the morning, they ate cereal and toast and chocolate malts.

"Ice cream," Zack commented. "Why am I not surprised?"

"You did a fair bit of surprising me a couple of hours ago," Anna said, forking egg off her plate. "I thought I'd taxed you to the limit, but you're a very...quick healer."

"Healer?" He smiled, his pillow-mussed hair tangled above his heavy-lidded eyes like a young boy's. He was wearing only his jeans; she, only his wrinkled denim shirt. "No one has ever called me a quick healer before." As soon as he'd said the words, he could have slapped himself. Why on earth had he referred to other sexual experiences? "Anna, I didn't mean—"

"Relax, Mr. Romantic Policeman," Anna said softly, amusement lighting her eyes. "I know what you meant. Whoever and whatever made you the man you are right now, I'm grateful to. And I know you would never be crass or thoughtless...*particularly* after the last few hours."

Zack cleared his throat, embarrassed. "Please. My sensibilities."

She left her chair and went to him, cradling him in her arms and rubbing her smile at the base of his throat. She had been away from him for far too long. Her lips trailed along the smooth skin of his shoulder, scattering kisses. His spoon clattered to the floor.

"Shhh," Anna cautioned, still smiling against his skin. "You'll wake Carrie."

"Oh, *now* you worry about waking Carrie," Zack muttered, feeling his heartbeat kick into second gear. "If you will remember, just a little while ago I had to put my hand over your mouth because—"

Anna put an end to the lecture by attacking him. There was no other word for it; it was a frontal attack with all the ammunition she had. She couldn't help herself. Life was far more wonderful than she could have ever dreamed; making love was wonderful; Zack was wonderful. And at that moment it seemed like nothing could ever go wrong, not when it came to Zack and Anna and the magic they made together.

Their ice cream melted into syrup. But it was sacrificed for a good cause.

Eight

When Zack opened his eyes much later that morning, Anna was gone. There was, however, a note left in red lipstick on her mirror.

"Good morning. Come and find me."

It wasn't going to be difficult to find her, since Zack could hear pots and pans clanging downstairs in the kitchen. He looked past the lipstick note at his own reflection and winced. He was not very pretty this morning, and to top things off, he had a hickey on his neck. Oh, if the boys at the precinct could see him now.

And speaking of his buddies in Los Angeles, Zack realized he hadn't called in once since he had left California. Captain Todd was going to keep him filled in on Pappy's progress, not to mention keeping him up-to-date on the progress tracking down the shooter. Feeling a little guilty about forgetting his life in L.A., Zack used the phone on the nightstand and called the captain's extension at the precinct. When Todd answered, he sounded every bit as irritable as the last time Zack had talked to him. Some things never changed.

"*What?*" Todd barked. Whether he was talking to the governor or to one of the baby-faced police cadets, his tone was always the same. Cranky.

Zack grinned, feeling much more patient with the old guy now that Anna was in his life. "Captain, you sound bright and cheerful as always. You are the sunshine in my life. What's up?"

"Daniels? Daniels, is that you? I told you to call in every day. Where the hell did you disappear to?"

"Hey, you *told* me to disappear. Uh...sir." Then, a horrible thought occurred. "Why? Have you been trying to find me? Is Pappy all right? He was doing okay when I left—"

"Pappy's on the mend. He even came into work for a couple of hours this morning, against doctor's orders, I might add. He's a stickler for duty. It's scary how much alike you two are. So where are you?"

Zack decided to evade the question. "I'm lost, far, far away from Los Angeles. And what's more, I *like* being lost."

"Well, don't get too attached to your freedom," Todd told him brusquely. "We caught the punk who shot Pappy yesterday. Now I don't need to worry about you playing the Lone Ranger and getting yourself in hot water. So say goodbye to your vacation, pack your bags and get back here."

For an instant Zack couldn't move. *Get back here.* He hadn't expected to hear that. Not this soon. His heart stopped.

"*Did you hear me?*" Todd shouted.

Zack winced, holding the phone away from his ear. "You don't need to yell. I can hear you."

"What's with you? I just gave you a reprieve from your exile. You can come home, Daniels. I'll put you back to work the minute you get here. *That* should make you happy."

Zack didn't feel happy. He felt sick.

"I can't leave," he said haltingly. "Not yet. Not...this soon."

There was a stunned silence on the other end of the line. "Is this Zack Daniels?" the captain boomed incredulously. "My very own pain in the—"

"Yes," Zack snapped, raking his hand impatiently through his hair. "This *is* Zack Daniels, and I haven't had a vacation for four years, captain. Don't you think it's about time you gave me a break?"

"Are you on some kind of medication? Do you have a fever?"

"I'm fine! I'm just not ready to strap on my gun again. What's the big deal?"

"The big deal," Todd said, in the tone of one speaking to the mentally impaired, "is that you are a cop and you need to come home and do cop *things*. It's what the good people of California pay you for."

Silence. Zack wondered if the captain could hear him grinding his teeth. Finally he decided to end the conversation before Todd called those nice young men in the clean white coats to come and take him to a mental hospital. "Captain, just cut me a little slack here, okay? I don't want to explain, and I don't want to come home."

"What? *Ever?*"

"Well, of course not *ever*. I'll come home, just not until..." he paused, closing his eyes tiredly. What could he say? He'd be back when he damn well felt like it? "Look, is there something in particular you need me for? If not, if it's business as usual down there, I'd appreciate some more time."

"Good grief," Todd said blankly. "I need to put out a missing person report. You can't *possibly* be Zack Daniels."

"Funny. I'll be back soon. I know I have responsibilities and I'll take care of them. I just need a few more days. Maybe another...another week or so."

"Hang on one minute," Todd said. "I have to look out the window and check if hell has frozen over."

One of Zack's strengths, or at least, something that had always been very convenient for him, was his ability to remain isolated. He could enjoy people, places and things, without actually letting them affect his emotions. This made not only his job easier but his personal life, as well. Be it an apartment, a relationship, whatever; he never had any trouble moving on to something new. As long as he had his job to provide his very own reason to live, he was content with his lot in life, whatever that lot might be. Rarely did his emotions give him cause for grief. Granted, had he lost Pappy, he would have hurt and hurt badly, but every cop knew the score when it came to the likelihood of living long enough to collect a full retirement. It was an iffy proposition. Besides, you certainly didn't become a cop for the money or benefits. You became a cop because anything else would have left you aching for fulfillment.

But right now Zack didn't want to be a cop. He wanted to be an architect, a stockbroker, contractor, something that would leave him sixteen hours out of every day to be with Anna in a seaside town called Grayland Beach. Unfortunately, he knew himself fairly well. He would miss the cop thing. He would miss the excitement. He would miss the feeling that he was truly making a difference in the world. It was something he was compelled to do, something that he knew he was good at. When it came to his job, he knew he was right where he was destined to be.

Long ago Zack had decided that there were many things in life worth dying for. Up until now, he had never given much thought to the things in life that were worth living for. Things had changed. Fate had taken a hand when he'd been locked in a basement with a tawny-haired, blue-eyed girl who was definitely worth living for. This called for him to develop a brand-new value system. Captain Todd, challenges, dancing on a tightrope between safety and danger...all those things had slipped way down on his priority scale. And though he would never admit it to anyone, Zack Daniels was scared. Having something to lose was a revelation. Having something to lose raised the stakes dramatically.

Being a cop was a great adventure, but not the ultimate adventure as he had always thought. Falling in love was. Discovering this bit of wisdom, however, didn't bring him much clarity. He needed Anna, he needed his work and he needed oxygen. In that order.

Quite simply, he had never been so confused in his entire life.

Anna was cooking.

She looked very good when she was cooking, Zack thought. She wore a silky blue wraparound kimono the same vivid color as her eyes. Her feet were looking festive in a pair of fuzzy bunny slippers sporting pink pom-poms on the heels.

"Hey, you," he called softly from the doorway.

She turned, her face breaking into a dazzling smile. Her long, long hair turned with her, swirling, sparkling, catching every beam of sunlight in the room. She was washed in light, he thought. So pretty. Her fresh, clean skin was luminous, shining from within. She wore not a speck of makeup and needed not a speck.

"Hey you, yourself," she said. She was wearing an oven mitt on her right hand, and waved it happily at him. "Long time no see. Almost thirty whole minutes."

Then Zack noticed something else that sparkled. Anna's eyes were shimmering with a veil of tears, which killed the sweet romance of the entire picture. His heart leaped into his throat, his mind was a cacophony of alarm bells. He flew across the kitchen, seizing her shoulders in his hands. "Anna? You're crying? You're *crying*. What's wrong?"

"No, I'm fine," she told him, earnest and touched by his intense reaction. "Zack, don't look so panicked. There are other reasons to cry besides being sad."

"Like what?" Zack asked, still off balance. "Pain? Pain! Are you in pain?"

"I'm…not…in…pain," she told him, carefully enunciating every word. Then she smiled, her fingers doing an eensy-weensy finger crawl up the placket of his white chambray shirt. "Here's something else you don't know about me. I don't cry much when I'm sad, but the tears come pretty freely when I'm happy. I know, I'm weird. Weird and happy."

"Then…" Zack struggled to understand, taking her in his arms and hugging her fiercely. "I'm to blame? But it's an okay thing, because they're happy tears?"

"Entirely," she said, her voice muffled against his chest. "You've sent my endorphins on a wonderful ride, Mr. Romantic Policeman. I was making you my famous sour cream breakfast cake, and *voilà!* The tears just started to flow. Be grateful you didn't come in here five minutes ago when I was giggling, too. You would have really thought I was nuts."

"You *are* a little strange." Zack sighed, patting her absently on the back. "But that's okay. If you're crying because you're happy, I won't have to kill anyone on your behalf."

She pulled back, staring at him curiously. "Would you do that?"

"Yes," he said without hesitation. "If someone was a threat to you, yes."

"Oh, my." Anna looped her arms around his neck, planting a kiss on his chin. "I'll have to be careful with you, won't I?"

"Immensely," Zack said meekly, heaving a great sigh. "I'm delicate where you're concerned. Handle me with tender loving care…or, if you'd rather, just *handle* me." He grinned, showing a flash of his usual bravado. "I've discovered I'm basically a carnal fellow where you're concerned."

"And you were pious and innocent back in Los Angeles? Led a monk's life?"

"Oh, yes."

"Never a single wild fling?"

He shook his head emphatically. "Oh, *no.*"

She grinned, loving the combination of wicked silvery eyes tucked into an angelic expression. Zack was an irresistible mixture of cherub and mischievous imp, emphasis on mischievous. She wriggled against him, luxuriating in the newfound freedom they had found together. Making love was an amazing liberator. "I hate to tell you this, but I have to leave you for a little while today."

His lower lip stuck out immediately. Already he didn't like this plan. "Why?"

"Because Kyle called a while ago and told me he was coming over at noon to talk to me. He didn't give me a chance to say no before he hung up. I don't think it's a good idea for me to be here, so I arranged to meet Carrie for lunch. I'm sorry to do this to you, but I'd like to ask you a little favor."

Since this favor seemed to involve Anna being away from him, Zack said immediately, "I'm sorry, I can't. It's impossible."

"You don't even know what the favor is yet."

"I'm afraid you're going to ask me to be civil to Kyle. Some things are simply not within my power." He smiled sweetly. "*Now* what should we talk about?"

His charm surrounded her, weaving a sweet, sexy spell. Anna had a wild impulse to use the kitchen table for something other than eating breakfast cake. Which she probably would have done had she not been pressed for time. She contented herself with a long, lingering kiss that instantly heated her blood to boiling. "Do me this little favor," she

whispered against his lips. "When Kyle gets here, don't kill
him. Just…try and open his eyes a little. Carrie's the best
thing that has ever happened to him. *Pleeeease?*"

"Evil woman," Zack muttered, his eyes dark with passion. "You know I can't refuse you anything."

"You won't hurt him?"

"Not even a little. But before you go—"

"I'm going to be late." She grinned, pushing him away
firmly. Her expression was positively joyous. In fact, she
felt joyous from inside out. "I need to shower and get ready.
The only problem is that I need someone to wash my back.
I know I'm asking a lot of favors from you this morning,
but…do you think you could manage that?"

Zack smiled at her with bright-eyed anticipation. "Oh,
yes. I love to be useful."

Zack had expected a less-than-pleasant encounter with
good old Kyle. No matter how you cut it, he didn't like the
guy.

Then Kyle walked in the house and Zack saw the misery
in his face. The man was hurting and didn't even bother to
hide the fact. Grudgingly Zack thought he'd give the guy a
break. He knew intuitively that Kyle was not aching for
Anna. He was missing Carrie.

"I'll fix you a sandwich," Zack said, leading Kyle back
to the kitchen. "Anna had a lunch date planned with Carrie,
so she left you to me."

Kyle only sighed and shrugged, taking this in stride. What
Anna was doing or not doing suddenly seemed not to matter
to him. On that basis, Zack began to like him just a little
bit more. But just a *little* bit.

"Carrie has been gone from my life for less than two
days," Kyle said morosely, straddling a kitchen chair backward while Zack searched the cupboards for peanut butter.
"And she's left a gaping, empty wound. Why are humans

so damn stupid? They never know what's important until it's gone."

"The human condition," Zack pronounced wisely. He liked to think he himself knew exactly what was important, without going through the suffering like Dr. Doolittle.

"I guess Carrie's staying here for a while?"

Zack gave him a look over his shoulder. "Only until she finds her own place."

"Oh, hell." Kyle's chin slumped to his knuckles on the chair back. "She's really doing this, isn't she? She's done with me."

"Can you blame her?" Zack asked, his head deep in the refrigerator. "Where the heck is the jam? Oh, there. Good. Anyway, like I said, Carrie isn't the one responsible for this. You're the one that turned schizo on her. What's the matter with you? She's wonderful, smart, funny...everything you could want. How could you possibly take a woman like her for granted?"

"I don't know," Kyle said glumly. "I guess I panicked. It's been me and my work for so long, I suddenly started thinking how many changes I was in for. I didn't know if I would *like* those changes. I live according to a routine— black coffee and dry toast for breakfast, head off to work at 8:00 a.m., go home at 5:30 p.m., eat a TV dinner and watch the news. Then I go to bed and the whole thing starts over again."

"That's horrible," Zack told him, repulsed. "Why on earth wouldn't you want a little excitement? Don't you get sick of living alone?"

"Don't *you?*" Kyle countered. "You're not exactly a spring chicken, and you're still a bachelor. You must like it that way."

"My life is different," Zack muttered, slathering peanut butter on bread with a heavy hand. "I'm a cop. I have constant challenges, I never know what will happen on any given day. I tell you, I've got a great…well, a really good…I've got an okay life.''

"Oh, *that* sounds like a contented man talking.''

Zack slapped Kyle's sandwich flat on the table, not bothering with plates. Then he sat down, buying himself some time while he munched on his Wonder bread lunch. "I thought I was happy,'' he said finally, a more somber note in his voice. "I thought I was the luckiest guy alive. Then I met Anna, and nothing else seemed to matter. My value system is in serious revolt.''

Kyle nodded understandingly. "Yeah, I know what you mean. When Carrie walked out of my life, she took my life with her. I'm lost. The idea of living without her is killing me.''

Zack shook his head. "You're a damned idiot. I suspected you might be from the moment I met you, and now you're proving it. Are you just going to sit back and cry in your beer the rest of your days?''

"Like I have a choice? I hurt her, Zack. She won't forgive that. Women and elephants *never* forget.''

"That's asinine. You know damn well you've got a *choice.* Do you love her?''

"Hell, yes, I love her. But it's too late. I blew it.''

Zack rolled his eyes "For a minute we were getting along here, but now you're starting to bug me again. Look, I don't know you real well, but you seem to be a normal kind of guy who pretty much accepts whatever life gives you. You've never fought against the routine, never made yourself stretch until it hurt.'' He paused, then slapped his free hand hard on the table. "Do you have any idea what the temperature of a dead body is?''

Kyle stared at him. "Are you kidding?''

Zack continued stubbornly, undeterred. "The temperature of a dead body is seventy-two degrees. The climate-controlled temperature of most homes is seventy-two degrees. Kyle, when we get that comfortable, when we dig ourselves into a rut that deep, *we might as well be dead.* If we don't get out of our comfort zones now and again, we hardly know we're alive. You've got to push yourself past your routine, soak in new ideas and new ways of living. Just because they're unfamiliar doesn't mean they're wrong. It's the only way to really live. So what if Carrie walked out on you? You deserved it. You were a complete jerk.''

"Thank you," he said irritably.

"So *stop* being a jerk already. Convince her that your life is meaningless without her. Sweep her off her feet. Humble yourself. Do whatever the hell is necessary to have her in your life. *Whatever* is necessary.''

Kyle was silent for a long moment. Then, with a strange catch in his voice, he said, "You're right. I've been so blind. And my damned routine isn't vital, it's just what I'm used to. Without Carrie I'm never going to be the man I could be. I'll be seventy-two degrees for the rest of my life, and seventy-two degrees when I'm dead and gone. I won't even know the difference.''

"Finally, he sees the light." Feeling rather smug, Zack finished off the last of his sandwich. "Damn, I'm good.''

Kyle cleared his throat self-consciously, loathe to ask for advice but having no real choice. "So tell me…if you were me—''

"What a horrible thought.''

"If you *were* me, how would you sweep Carrie off her feet?''

"Give me a break. You're a big boy. You made her fall in love with you once, you can do it again. Dazzle her. Apologize profusely to her. Wine and dine her. Send her a dozen roses every day for the rest of your life. Remember the motto. Whatever it takes.''

Kyle considered this, drawing finger circles on the table top. "I can do that. Probably.''

"Kyle, have a little confidence. You're…all right. You're

not a *complete* weasel. You're just a little inexperienced when it comes to battling for what you want.''

''What about you?'' Kyle asked quietly, looking up. ''Is that what you did with Anna? All these years I've watched so many men take one look at her and fall hard, but no one even came close to succeeding until you came along. I guess that was part of my problem. I was her best friend until she met you, the first one she called when she was lonely or had a problem. I guess I was jealous of being replaced.''

''You're still her friend, you know that. But if you're really honest with yourself, aren't you the one who changed on her? Aren't *you* the one who found a new best friend when you fell in love with Carrie?''

''Maybe,'' Kyle conceded reluctantly. ''I never thought of it that way. I'm getting to be more of a jerk every minute, aren't I?''

Zack nodded enthusiastically, though he said, ''That's your call.''

They talked for another thirty minutes, mostly concerning the art of seducing a woman you had wronged. Kyle listened intently, right down to actually taking notes. He was in short supply of imagination, but he was capable of following specific instructions. ''I'm inspired,'' Kyle told Zack, pushing his chair back from the table. ''Unfortunately I have a date with a pregnant poodle, so I have to go. You're not a bad guy, Daniels.''

''I *can* be,'' Zack said honestly, trailing him to the door. ''But if you're not interested in Anna romantically, you're probably in no danger.''

Kyle paused at the front door, giving Zack a firm handshake. ''You know, I'm glad you obviously care about her so much. After that abominable childhood she had, she deserves only good things. When I think about all the mental and physical abuse she went through, I can hardly believe she turned out as loving and well-adjusted as she is. Hell, she was in intensive care in the hospital three or four times before she was eight years old. But I'm sure you know all that. She's a survivor, isn't she?''

Zack's heart coughed and stalled with Kyle's pronouncement. Fortunately, he was an old hand at projecting calm understanding while his vital signs were off the chart. It was a cop thing. Being a male, and a possessive one at that, he didn't want to tell Kyle how little he knew about Anna's past. Foster homes, that's all he knew. He took a deep breath and steadied himself. "It's not something she talks about much."

"It's nothing I'd want to think about, either. It's a credit to her adoptive parents that Anna's as well-adjusted as she is. They were completely devoted to her, both of them. They did everything in their power to compensate for the miserable beginning she had in life. When they were killed in the accident, I was afraid she'd be destroyed, but she dealt with it. Sometimes I wonder just how much one person has to go through in this world. It goes without saying that it isn't fair."

"Life seldom is." Zack's expression remained clean and still. But the blood in his veins felt cool, and every word Kyle said echoed like gunshots in his ears. "She's lucky to have friends like you."

Kyle shrugged, his face hard with unpleasant thoughts. "If you ask me, nothing makes up for her past." He paused, then added, "She doesn't need to be hurt again. Ever. But I guess you feel the same way."

Zack nodded. "Yes." The one little word was all he could manage.

After Kyle left, Zack walked into the parlor and literally dropped on the couch. His head was hurting, his heart was hurting, every cell in his body felt wounded. It was as if everything she had gone through, he was somehow feeling himself.

He was beginning to understand what he had done. By leading Anna into a relationship with him, he had put her into the position of being vulnerable once again. Worse, he couldn't escape the haunting fear that hurting her was inevitable. He knew what kind of man he was—not a bad guy, but definitely his father's son. Not a man likely to be domesticated. Zack hadn't realized the consequences of giving in to his passions. He'd allowed himself to get lost in the moment, to tell his conscience to take a flying leap.

He wanted to scream and rail at fate, to tell the Almighty just what he thought of Him. It wasn't that he had any illusions about the world he lived in. A cop often came into contact with people who were either abused as children or who were abusing their own children. It was a sobering education. It had saddened him, it had made him angry, but it had never terrified him.

He was terrified now.

He didn't know the ending of his love story. He *did* know that until he met Anna, he'd been living the life he was best suited for. He did what he could for other people, but he'd never promised more than he could deliver. Rarely had he been burdened with thoughts of conscience, because he had done his best to present himself honestly, warts and all.

But *now,* now the world was a different place, and Zack was a different man. He felt somehow he had deceived Anna by allowing her to think he was good for her. He wasn't sure what she expected from their relationship, but obviously her friends and her home were terribly important to her. She'd gone so long without security or love in her life. Then she had found her parents, and the sun had shone on her for a short while. But instead of having a happy ending, the ending she deserved, she'd faced another soul-wrenching loss. It was like a cruel fate was telling her, "Here, enjoy this for a little while. But don't get too attached, because nothing lasts forever."

Zack had no idea how she survived it all, but the woman he'd met at Appleton's was incredibly strong and seemingly heart-whole. Then along came Zack Daniels, and suddenly Anna was put in the position of being a victim. Again.

He sat there for the longest time, trying to come up with a way to solve it all. He felt like a man facing a thousand-piece jigsaw puzzle with the clock ticking down. Finding Anna had been a miracle. Yet, as far as he was concerned, he was the least likely man to deserve a miracle.

Finally he understood how wrong he'd been. He'd seen what he wanted and gone after it, never dreaming he would fall in love in the process. Anna wasn't *separate,* like he was. She belonged to a home, friends, hopes and dreams. Zack belonged to…nothing. His apartment had never been a home. His friends had never been his family. His work had been the closest thing to happiness he had ever found.

Until Anna.

Zack bowed his head, burying his face in his hands. He'd always known what his life would be. He would be free, independent and unchained, today, tomorrow and always. Free.

Free. That word had never sounded less appealing.

"What do you mean, he took *notes?*" Anna asked Zack.

They were seated in the back of a dimly lit restaurant, the sort of place where they used real napkins, real crystal and real linen tablecloths. Being a single man, Zack was more accustomed to hamburgers or pizza, paper napkins and a cold beer, but tonight Anna had mischievously decided to "stake out" the restaurant where Kyle was meeting Carrie for dinner. As per Zack's instructions, Kyle had sent Carrie three dozen roses that afternoon, with a handwritten note that begged her to meet him at "their" restaurant. They had come here on their first date, and Zack had told Kyle that women always liked a nice show of sentiment.

"I swear," Zack replied, "the man took notes. He didn't want to make any mistakes." He was doing his best to disguise the emotional upheaval he was battling, but he was aching and tense from the effort of projecting a lighthearted mood. He wasn't ready yet to face anything close to reality. And so he'd obligingly dressed for dinner in black slacks, a pewter silk shirt and matching tie, an outfit he'd purchased that afternoon in Grayland Beach. His appearance suggested a man with a smooth veneer of experience and sophistication, a man at peace with himself and the world. Appearances lied.

"It's almost like you and Kyle are bosom buddies," Anna replied teasingly. She'd been very grateful when she returned from lunch with Carrie and found no corpses in her house. Still, she wanted to track Kyle and Carrie's progress personally, which necessitated the visit to the restaurant. They had come early and had asked to be seated in the back of the room, behind an immense potted palm. Fortunately, there was just enough room between the rubbery green leaves for Anna to spy. It was a fine new game to play with her romantic policeman. She would have brought binoculars if she thought she could have gotten away with it. Then she could have read their lips.

Kyle and Carrie hadn't arrived yet, so there was plenty of time for Anna to cheerfully drool over her partner in crime…and in love. Again, binoculars would have been nice. Kind of like a big-screen close-up of the man who controlled the rhythm of her heart. Anna loved the combination of masculinity and sexiness he radiated in his sleek, stylish clothes. She was acutely sensitive to every movement he made, every ripple of muscle beneath his silk shirt, every flicker of his deep-set gray eyes. Suddenly Anna was of two minds. She wanted to watch Kyle's progress with Carrie; she also wanted to take her man home and ravish him mercilessly. Pull off his tie, loosen his shirt, tangle her fingers in his hair and revel in the man beneath the polish. She thought he might like that. And she knew she would adore it.

"So do you think this will work?" she asked, dreamily focused on Zack's lips.

Zack shrugged, smiling faintly. "I hope so, for Carrie's sake. I guess we'll know soon." Even while fighting his inner demons, he couldn't take his eyes off the woman seated opposite him at the small table. Anna, too, had worn something fancy for the occasion, and it was the first time Zack had seen her in a dress. If Anna could look good in a kimono and bunny slippers, she positively dazzled when she was dressed to kill. She wore a short, black-sequined halter-top dress, shimmering sheer black nylons and strappy heels so high, they brought the top of her head even with Zack's eyes. Dangling black pearl earrings flashed through her long, honey-gold hair, reaching almost to her shoulders and adding a gypsy-like touch to an otherwise elegant outfit. She stopped his heart.

Naturally men had stared at her when they'd walked in, forks paralyzed in midair. Zack could swear a hush fell over the room. Their waiter had visited their table five times already, and they hadn't finished their hors d'oeuvres yet. A second waiter hovered nearby, refilling their water glasses each time they took a sip. And the beaming maître d' had actually come over twice, encouraging them to take their time and enjoy a long, leisurely meal. Zack could hardly figure out who to punch first.

"Why on earth are you scowling at our waiter?" Anna asked curiously. "He's been very attentive."

"There's something about attentive waiters that makes me claustrophobic," Zack muttered, distracted by her appearance, his own thoughts and the googly eyed males hovering nearby. "Not to mention the attentive busboy and the attentive maître d'. Now I know how you felt in Appleton's."

"I promise to catch you if you swoon." Anna cocked her head sideways, staring at him with a little furrow between her brows. "Zack? Are you all right? You seem awfully preoccupied tonight. What's wrong?"

"Nothing's wrong," Zack said, taking a long swallow of water while he collected himself. Then, when the young kid with the water pitcher instantly appeared, he gave him a warning look and said flatly, *"Go away."*

"That wasn't very nice," Anna said, watching the busboy run for cover.

"He was looking at you."

"I didn't notice." A little smile played with the corners of her mouth. Her lips were the most amazing color tonight, a rich burgundy with sheer gloss. Kissable, flirtable, shaped for pure, sweet love.

"I did." Zack had a hundred desperate thoughts of what those lips could do to him, and vice versa. The strain was evident in his voice. "I've just discovered the pain of going out in public with Venus. I can't count the number of eyes focused on you."

"You're exaggerating. I'm just another face in the crowd," Anna said, looking at him cross-eyed to prove her point. In fact, she truly hadn't noticed anyone looking at her. She was too busy noticing the man she was with. Putting a tie on Zack was rather like putting a pretty little bow around the neck of a sleek, dangerous lion. "So tell me, what did you do to make Kyle be civil?"

"I didn't do anything," he said. He reached across the table for no other reason than to simply touch her hand. He couldn't be this close to her without touching her. It was impossible. "Kyle had a wake-up call when Carrie walked out on him. Sometimes you need to lose someone before you realize how important they are." He heard his own words and closed his eyes briefly. He didn't want to be on the receiving end of that experience. "Hopefully they'll manage a happy ending. Change is always a little scary."

Anna smiled faintly, distracted by their intertwined hands on the cream-colored tablecloth. It seemed she would never become accustomed to his touch. No matter how innocent, no matter how casual, it always took her breath away. "Well, you managed to help him see the light. Carrie actually looked happy tonight when she was getting ready. It was good to see her smile again." She gave him a look of pure, blue-eyed temptation. "I owe you, Mr. Romantic Policeman. Maybe you can be thinking about how I can return the favor."

"Don't do that," Zack told her darkly. When she wasn't flirting, she was charming and appealing and sweetly seductive. When she *was* flirting, no man within fifty miles stood a snowball's chance in hell of remaining immune. And Zack was a lot closer than fifty miles. "Not unless you'd like to forget about dinner and go home. *Now.*"

"If I didn't know better," Anna replied innocently, "I'd think you have something on your mind besides nourishment."

Softly, "Oh, yes."

Anna was actually considering leaving the restaurant then and there, when she noticed Kyle and Carrie walking in. Kyle looked a little awkward in a three-piece suit, as if he might have tied the tie a bit too tight. Carrie was in a gauzy, scoop-necked dress that floated around her knees when she walked. Kyle looked intense and determined. She looked carefree, breezy and untouchable.

"Look," Anna whispered to Zack, nodding her head in Carrie and Kyle's direction. "The play begins. Doesn't she look lovely?"

"Oh, yes," Zack said quietly, his hungry gaze devouring Anna's exquisite face. "She looks…perfect."

Twice their waiter came for their menus and twice they shooed him away. Their eyes peered over the tops of the menus while they watched Kyle and Carrie shamelessly. It seemed to go well, though Anna said more than once she wished she could overhear them. Kyle did quite a bit of talking, actually, taking a piece of paper out of his jacket pocket at one point and studying it while Carrie visited the powder room. Anna barely stifled her giggles. "Zack, you were telling the truth," she crowed. "He's reading his *notes*. My goodness, he's trying hard. He's making progress, don't you think?"

"I think so," Zack replied quietly, his eyes shadowed as he watched Kyle stand politely when Carrie returned to the table. A tendril of Kyle's hair was sticking up at his crown, like a cowlick that had broken its bonds of hair gel. Carrie smiled faintly at him, seeing the cowlick and the linen napkin snagged on his belt. Kyle reached out and touched her cheek, very briefly. They had the look of two people who had been together a long time, a man and a woman who could understand and anticipate the other's emotions. They had come to love one another honestly, as a man and a woman with human frailties and imperfections. The fact that they belonged together was obvious. Looking at them, you knew instinctively that they would last, that beneath the confusion and sorting out of very human mistakes, they were committed. And somehow, as a couple they added up to much more than they ever could have been by themselves. The picture they made was an emblem of honesty, forgiveness and kindness. They were companions.

Zack knew what it was to be a lover, but he'd never been anyone's companion. That prospect had always left him cold. But now, with Anna, the privilege of being her companion seemed to embody the ultimate achievement. An achievement that seemed so very far beyond his reach.

He closed his eyes briefly, tired of envying Kyle and Carrie, tired of sharing Anna with the ogling men at the restaurant, tired of eating food he barely tasted. He didn't want dessert. He didn't want to wait until Kyle and Carrie finished their meal to leave the restaurant. More than anything, he didn't want to think anymore. He only wanted to feel. "Anna?"

She was still watching her friends. "Hmm?"

Very softly, "I want you."

At that, she looked at him full on, reading the simmering emotion in his eyes. She realized that her body had been missing his in more ways than she could begin to count. She ached. She wanted to be in a place where they were free, where there were no prying eyes.

Without another word she pushed her chair back from the table. "We can go out the back. I want to go home, too."

Nine

Carrie didn't come home that evening. Zack and Anna barely noticed.

They arrived at Anna's lovely, whimsical Victorian after a curiously silent ride home. Walking up the floodlit front steps, Zack saw many things he hadn't noticed before. All those details Anna had painstakingly added to the exterior put her own stamp on the precious thing she had finally achieved—a home. Zack thought he understood far better now how very much Anna loved this place, and why. Few people had to fight such a long, lonely battle for a place to belong. No wonder she treasured this house. Like Anna, it was one-of-a-kind, tangible proof that she would never again be at the mercy of the winds of fate. She belonged here.

But I don't, Zack thought numbly. All that he truly was, he'd left back in Los Angeles. He was only borrowing a few precious moments from Anna's life, pretending it was permanent. Beyond that, the future was ominously blank.

Anna was an amazing example of beating the odds, a woman of strength and grace and resilience. Zack was a product of his environment, a man who had decided long ago not to try and be something he wasn't. He'd found his peace by expecting a great deal from himself in his work and treading cautiously when it came to his personal life. He knew what he was capable of, and he knew what things were beyond him. If he couldn't give one hundred percent, he wasn't going to play the game. That way he could tell himself he had learned something from his father's mistakes.

Anna knew Zack was lost in his thoughts. She waited until they walked into the shadowed interior of the house, turning on a single, stained-glass lamp in the entry hall. Zack's brown, chiseled face was hazily illuminated with a soft rainbow of sheer color.

"You look so far away," she whispered, wondering at the deep shadows in his beautiful eyes.

"I am," he replied in a hollow voice. "At least three feet too far."

Anna expected him to move then, to take her in his arms and make the sensual magic she craved. Strangely, he stayed where he was, staring at her. "What's going on in you?" she asked softly. "Has something happened?"

He gave himself a minute, tugging his tie off. "Something happens all the time."

He was starting to scare her now. Anna remained rooted to the floor, a succession of confused emotions flashing across her expressive face. Her festive black dress glittered cheerfully with the rise and fall of her breathing, looking strangely out of place in the heavy atmosphere. "What can I do to make you smile again?" she said finally, the words barely audible.

Zack continued to stare at her long and hard. Then, with his jaw clenched and his eyes narrowed, he looped his tie over Anna's head, holding each end and pulling it taut. He drew her toward him, still holding her gaze. He said nothing, but his eyes were suddenly alive with a blazing need.

Anna wet her shaky lips with the tip of her tongue, her fingers splayed across the silky material of his shirt. Her throat felt dry and tight, and her heart was a trip-hammer in her chest. She'd never felt so immersed in elemental desire. In that instant she thought she understood. He was feeling only his most basic instincts. He was giving free rein to them, and the prospect of being the sole focus of his needs shook her to her core. This was about desire. And it was incredibly arousing, because she knew there was so much more between them than *just* sex.

"Love me," she whispered in an aching velvet voice.

"I do." Zack had never said that to a woman, he didn't even know if Anna realized he was speaking his heart. The moment was sharp-edged and acute, burned instantly and forever in his memory. There was thunder in his ears, a pulse jumping hard in his neck. He swore he could feel the earth breathing beneath his feet. "I do love you, Anna."

Her eyes softened. She was going to say something then, but Zack didn't give her a chance. His mouth slanted over hers with barely restrained power, drinking deeply from the siren's lips that had tempted him all evening. The explosion of feeling was instantaneous, his body hardening in the space of a heartbeat. He forced himself to drive every rational thought from his mind, concentrating only on this woman and this night.

Anna kicked off her shoes, still kissing him. Being almost as tall had been nice, but she would hate to take a tumble at this point and spend the night having a broken ankle set instead of in her bed with the man she loved. She scattered small kisses on his lips, everywhere. She clung to him with all her strength, wanting and giving in equal measure. In the back of her mind she recognized the sound of a button popping off. She pulled back and blinked at Zack, her lipstick smeared and her eyes wide. "Your new shirt," she gasped in dismay. "I've turned into a heathen. I need more practice to be adept. I'm sorry."

His lips tipped up in the faint question marks she loved. "*Adept?* Angel, you're more than I can handle already. If you were any more adept, it could kill me."

She dipped her chin and gave him a quizzical look, a hint of the devil in her baby blue eyes. "Am I a good student?"

He shook his head. "No. You're a good teacher. Don't you know that by now?"

Anna hesitated, caught by the ragged, strained quality in his voice. Something compelled her to gently press her lips against his hard brown cheek, her satin flesh absorbing the heat there. "What could I have possibly taught you?"

Zack took a long moment to answer. There was a whirlwind of anxiety and raw passion inside him, yet at the same time he felt an infinite tenderness. His emotions were no longer segregated into distinct areas, logical and predictable. He wanted her physically, he wanted her with his heart and soul. The long evening spent in a public place had not only intensified his yearning, but his vague, nameless anxiety, as well. Finally he held her face with his feverish hands, willing her to understand. "To be thankful," he said.

Anna smiled faintly, loving him with her soft eyes. "You're amazing, Mr. Romantic Policeman."

"Actually I'm going a little bit crazy." Zack hadn't realized it until now, but ever since his talk with Kyle, he had felt odd and unsettled. He wasn't a man who experienced fear often, only when it seemed that someone else might be hurt due to some mistake on his part. Tonight, as always, he willed everything to be all right. That was the way he had always approached life, the way he handled his job so successfully. He *forced* everything to go the way he thought it should.

What about now? his conscience whispered, unusually sensitive.

"You're doing it again," Anna whispered. "Your eyes…just like that, you go so far away. What's wrong?"

"Nothing. I'm not going anywhere, sweetheart." Very deliberately he closed his mind to his conscience, focusing for all he was worth on the more urgent needs of his body. He made yearning motions on her back, her shoulders, her hips, holding her, possessing her, memorizing the hollows and curves. He buried kisses in her hair, along the fragile curve of her neck and on the sensitive flesh below her collarbone. As his passion heated, he realized the moment felt oddly out of place in the prim little Victorian parlor. It was the sort of room where you received visitors, where you sat with your ankles crossed and your hands folded neatly in your lap. He had no desire to cross his ankles or keep his hands folded safely in his lap. "Anna, let me take you upstairs—"

"Upstairs? All the way upstairs?" Anna clung to Zack's shoulders, shuddering as she felt his palms slide beneath her dress, pushing it to her thighs. The combination of sheer nylons, warm skin and hungry fingers made her dizzy with wanting. In her mind she imagined this erotic ritual taking place in the ultraconservative Victorian era, defying their surroundings. *That* would have been wicked and daring and dangerous.

She loved the thought.

Zack's mind was a cacophony of emotion, his body cramped and hard with painful need. If he paused, he might remember how tenuous this situation was, how unpredictable the future. He didn't pause, he barely allowed himself the time to breathe. His mouth was raining kisses on her mouth, her hair, her silky eyelids. He wanted to love her everywhere. Everywhere. Now.

In her eyes, he saw clear, unvarnished emotion. She hid nothing; he knew it would never occur to her to be anything but open with her emotions and desires. Chills of urgency became like icy slivers in his nerves. His craving for possession was insatiable. He groaned, abandoning the last faint threads of his shredding willpower. Since first looking at her, it had been all he could manage to keep a stranglehold on his baser instincts. To abandon control was ecstasy.

They kissed in lost, fierce ways, their lips barely breaking contact while they muttered endearments and pleas and staggered toward the sofa. There was unrelenting darkness beyond the white-paned windows, but here in this barely lit room was heat and comfort for two hungry hearts who had finally come in from the cold. Hell could break loose in the midnight sky, the cold, uncertain world could shatter and dissolve around them, but they were safe on sacred ground.

Anna had been so careful all her life, with her time, her heart and her hope. Tonight, however, caution was only a vague memory, a burden she was relieved to abandon. Breathless, she sank down to the carved oak sofa, her dress pushed high and her silk-clad legs tangling around Zack's thighs. Inside she felt as if hot, sweet honey was seeping into her deepest parts. The only sound she heard was her own silent voice demanding that she become part of him, that she give herself to him.

Zack sank against her, fighting fire with fire. She was an erotic weight beneath his seeking body, an amazing source of security and mystery and release. His right hand cradled her head, trying to protect her from the lacquered hardwood edging the tufted velvet sofa. With his left hand he tried to find a bracing point so neither of them took a header off the couch, all the while rocking and pressing against her body like a man possessed...which he was. One thing about those sadistic Victorians, they sure knew how to make a couch uncomfortable. Even a rugged and innovative cop from Oakland couldn't fight a Victorian sofa.

Out of sheer desperation, they found the carpeted floor. Here they found freedom to move and roll and explore the feelings of wild abandonment. A bed suddenly became mundane, something only conservative folks insisted on. They were different. Exultant and artless, Anna was framed by the glorious halo of her hair. He kissed her sweetly, like a man would kiss an untouched angel; he kissed her hard and long, like a man would kiss a wanton temptress he was trying to tame.

Her nylons disappeared, and Zack felt a hard shock when he realized she had been wearing absolutely nothing beneath her dress. He clenched his jaw, staring down at her lovely, flushed face. "You humble me," he said hoarsely. "I want to give everything to you. I want to take you places you've never been…"

There was something in his expression that touched her heart, something vulnerable and sweet. Her shaky fingers framed his face, while an even shakier smile trembled on her kiss-swollen lips. "Then take me," she whispered. "I want to be right there with you, everywhere you go. Anywhere."

Zack was too emotional to be proficient. Experiences of the past were irrelevant. Tonight he had nothing to go on but his love for this woman, and that was an experience he'd never had before. It felt holy and pure to him, despite the intensity of his physical response to her. Their lips and hands made magic together. Damp, with lithe and limber motions, they explored well the full length of their bodies. Anna seemed to welcome everything—his driving kisses, his frantic hands, and his body that instinctively began to thrust with a primitive movement. And still she looked at him with restless smiles and a feverish expression that clearly said, *It's not enough.*

Yet Zack paused, for a moment looking oddly young and vulnerable. "Say it," he said softly. Never before had he wanted to hear the words, *I love you.* Never once. And on the few occasions he *had* heard those words, unbidden, he had soon departed, like all the hounds in hell were hot on his trail. Allowing a woman to need him had always been anathema to him. His mother had needed his father, and received nothing in return but silence and loneliness.

But that was then and this was now. This night was a moment out of time, a place of magic that had no connection to the real world.

Anna's passion-filled eyes briefly questioned him, then understanding dawned. She took his hand, pressing it fiercely over her heart. "I love you."

A flush of heat stained his nose and cheeks like a little boy's sunburn. How could it be? And yet he knew she meant what she said, because Anna had never bothered to hide her feelings and never would. She was uncorrupted, clear-sighted and beautifully honest.

Zack's eyes suddenly shimmered, blurring the beautiful vision below him. What was this? Not tears, he thought, because he knew himself fairly well and was toughened by years of risky situations and heartbreaking realities. With the exception of the night his mother left his father, he couldn't think back to a single time in his life when he had cried. No, not tears. Something else was fogging his vision and tying his throat in a vicious, triple-looped lover's knot.

Wonderingly Anna gently touched a sparkling teardrop at the corner of his eye.

"The light hurts my eyes," he said hoarsely, referring to the thirty-five-watt bulb burning invisibly out in the entry hall. "It's very bright."

"As bright as the moon," Anna said softly, thinking how beautiful he was, how brilliant and sweet his expression. "Except there's no moon tonight."

"Don't be a smart aleck." He swallowed painfully, dipping his forehead down to rest against hers. For a moment they stayed like that, frozen, communicating with their spirits while deliberately prolonging the union of their bodies. Then Zack moved with a sudden groan, drinking deeply from her mouth. Almost instantly they were hot, frantic and close to delirium. The clothes that impeded them disappeared like magic, hanging here and there on furniture and lamps. It was a nice touch, Zack thought. Added spice to the Victorian theme.

Then he thought no longer.

Slowly, ever so slowly he sank into her, and the overwhelming physical sensations intensified with every second. He tilted her hips with his strong hands, wanting to get even deeper. *I want all of you.* He wasn't aware he had actually said the words aloud until she tucked one side of her mouth in a crooked smile and said breathlessly, ''I think you're about there. Ohhhhh, you feel so good to me…''

She climbed. The waves of pleasure began soft and gentle, then quickly grew strong. Anna felt greedy, wanting, wanting, wanting. Zack loved the passion in her face, the wild and complete abandonment she was able to achieve so effortlessly. She was made for love.

Zack took her by the heart and the mind and the body into a place that dazzled her with stars and sunshine and sugar-sweet release. He kept her suspended for a blinding space of time, prolonging the unearthly pleasure as long as he was humanly able. He had ways and means, and he used them all. He had never wanted to please a woman this much in his life. Every need she had, he wanted to fill. He wanted to be everything to her, her entire world.

Anna clung to him after, gasping and crying and telling him over and over she loved him. It was music to Zack's ears, every word she spoke filling the empty places in his soul.

I love you…

I love you…

Forever…

The first time they had made love, it had been so new and amazing she could barely take it all in. This time was different; this time they had pushed each other to the limits of their bodies and minds. Worlds of wonder had opened up to Anna. For the second time in her life she felt she had found a perfect home.

Time had ceased to be an accurate measure of the night. It might have been minutes later, it might have been hours later, when Anna opened her eyes, purred and stretched. The parlor was dark, a bit cool. She was covered only by Zack's brand-new shirt which was missing a button. He was stretched out on his side on the carpet, arm curled beneath his head, staring at her.

"Did you sleep?" she asked him in a soft, husky voice.

He shook his head, his expression unusually somber. "There's no time for sleep. I had important things to do."

"Such as...?"

"Memorizing things. The way you look when you're sleeping. The way your pulse throbs just beneath your ear. The beautiful frame your hair makes for your face, like a delicate cameo. It's so beautiful, with more shine than satin. I've never seen anything like it before. The world will never see your like again, Anna."

She studied him with fathomless blue eyes, a flush of love marking her cheeks and chin. "Have you ever thought what your children would look like? Have you thought about their eyes, their hair, if they would laugh like you or walk like you?"

In point of fact, he hadn't. That was a subject that had always been taboo for him. "Not really." Then, when he saw the curiosity in her expression, "Is that strange?"

"No, just...well, I always thought everyone else was like me, thinking about their babies and wondering what they would be like. It's human nature to want to leave something of yourself in the world when your time is over." She paused for an uncertain moment, wondering if she should say what was on her mind. Then she thought of the intimacies they had shared and decided their relationship was strong enough to allow her to be honest. Besides, it wasn't in her nature to hide her emotions. "Every time I look at you, I wonder what a child of yours would be like. A son, with black hair and those restless, stormy eyes of yours." She smiled faintly, reaching out her hand and touching his face. "I hope the world does see your like again, Mr. Romantic Policeman."

Zack was struck mute. His eyes grew even darker and deeper, his skin quickly becoming chilled. He never thought about children, because he sincerely doubted he would ever have any. He wasn't willing to walk out of the house every day, wave goodbye to his kids and his wife and wonder if it was the last time he would see them. His job wasn't frightening to him in the least—as long as it affected only him. If others were involved, it became terrifying. He would not, could not, hurt anyone else with the same careless disregard he had seen from his father so many times. As a cop, the man was a hero. As a husband and father, he was something else altogether. Zack had never been willing to make someone else pay the price of his own inherent inadequacies.

"It's late," he said abruptly.

Anna's brows drew together in a little frown. "Zack? I wasn't…I didn't mean…"

"I know. It's fine, really." Now Zack knew firsthand why a love affair was called an idyll. An idyll was when you pushed every logical thought from your mind and reacted only with your heart. It was a suspended moment in time when you pretended nothing could go wrong. It was fleeting and precious and fragile. He couldn't escape the sensation of his time with Anna running out, like sand in an hourglass.

Kyle and Carrie came over for breakfast, once again talking weddings. They were holding hands, seldom looking away from the other for too long. The sparkle was back in Carrie's eyes, and there was a new confidence and assurance in Kyle's demeanor. They walked into the house and brought with them a fresh breeze of newfound contentment.

Zack envied them that. He would never have figured he would covet the life of this rather ordinary and occasionally irritating veterinarian. He couldn't remember feeling bored in his own life, but neither did he know what it was to be content. There was always a new goal on the horizon, a new challenge to be met and conquered. He never relaxed, not really. If he did, he had the feeling he was letting someone down, somewhere, somehow. Again, just like his father. He couldn't do that.

During breakfast he barely took his eyes off Anna, drinking in the bright, vivid expressions on her beautiful face. When she laughed, she wrinkled her nose. There was a definite razor-burn on her cheeks. She glowed, just as Carrie glowed. If there was anything wrong in her world, you couldn't see it by looking at her.

Zack began to feel a little sick. He'd always known what he needed to do to solve his problems, and he'd always been capable of doing it. His principles were his guidelines. But how on earth could he ever solve this? A man of principle wouldn't be in this no-win situation in the first place.

His decisions no longer affected only him. He was facing the destruction of a lifetime's assumptions about himself and his role in the world. Actions that had always seemed heroic were now rather blurred and confusing. He had discovered, too late, that he was just as human as anyone else.

Not long after Kyle and Carrie left, there was a phone call for Zack. "I didn't realize anyone knew where you were," Anna said curiously, handing him the phone.

Zack looked up at her from the newspaper he was pretending to read. At least he wasn't holding it upside down. He was painfully preoccupied, intensely sensitive to the thick mood in the sunny kitchen. Anna's cheerful banter had ceased abruptly as soon as Kyle and Carrie had left. Apparently she *had* noticed his uncharacteristic reserve. What had happened to his much-touted ability to disguise his true thoughts and feelings? In the space of a few short days, he had become frighteningly easy to read. *Zing*, I'm happy. *Bam*, I'm depressed. *Hell, I'm confused.*

"Thanks." Smiling faintly at the wallpaper over her shoulder, he took the phone. He knew exactly who was calling. "Hello, Captain. Long time no talk."

"Stuff the fun and nonsense," Todd told him. "I haven't had my eight cups of coffee yet this morning, and I'm still irritable."

"And the sky is still blue. Some things never change," Zack muttered, his eyes following Anna as she put the breakfast dishes in the sink. The atmosphere in the room was awfully heavy for two people who were supposed to be in the throes of a romantic idyll. "How did you find this number, anyway?"

"*How* long have you been a cop, Daniels? Tracing calls is one of the things we do, remember? I'm sure it will all come back to you as you get back here. *Which*," he paused for emphasis, "will be, without argument, *today.*"

Zack took a good long time to answer. "No. Not today." Strangely, his voice lacked conviction. He watched Anna's shoulders stiffen as she worked at the sink with her back to him. "I'm still…I'm on vacation."

"Daniels, either your vacation or your job ended about one minute ago—take your pick. We need to get a statement from you before we can lock Pappy's shooter up and throw away the key. In person. First thing tomorrow morning—8:00 a.m."

Zack's eyes slowly closed. He felt hollow inside, scraped out by an age-old, rusted knife. A serrated rusted knife. "That's too soon. Look, I won't be much longer. It's not like I'm planning on staying here forever. Just…a couple of days or so."

A glass dropped in the sink, shattering. Still Anna kept her back to Zack, bracing her palms on either side of the sink. She was wearing a loose, white cotton sundress that foamed around her tanned, bare legs with a casual, flirtatious air at odds with the emotion crowding the kitchen. Her hair was tied with a narrow white ribbon at the base of her neck. It was still damp from showering that morning. All these details Zack memorized, filled with a frantic sense of impending doom. He realized he had just deliberately cut his own throat. *I'm not planning on staying here forever.* He knew it, and she knew it.

"I'm not kidding on this one," Todd shouted, hurting Zack's ears. "You want this guy to walk? What's happened to you? You're sure as hell not acting like a cop anymore. *Are* you still a cop?"

"Of course I'm still a cop," Zack fired back, stung. "And Pappy is still my partner, and I do care what happens. You *know* me, Captain. I'm not about to let anyone down." Famous last words...too little, too late.

"You'll be here tomorrow." It wasn't a question. It was a flat demand, and Todd slammed down the receiver before Zack could argue.

Zack stood to hang up the phone, moving in slow motion. He pushed his hands into the pockets of his jeans, keeping his back to Anna until he felt the touch of her hand on his shoulder.

"So tell me," she said tonelessly. "What was all that?"

Zack turned to face her. He had never seen her blue eyes look so dark or so deep. "That was Captain Todd, back in Los Angeles. He needs me to come home immediately. The guy who shot my partner has been arrested. I need to give a statement in court first thing tomorrow. It's something I can't get out of."

"Is that all?" she asked with a stiff, unconvincing smile. "Here I thought something terrible had happened. I know you have a job to do, Zack. You had a life before you met me. Right?"

She met this like she did everything in her life, Zack thought. Straight on and right between the eyes. He could see more than he wanted to in the stiffness of her posture,

the unnaturally high set of her head. He had taught her to
love him and she did. The pain they were both feeling was
a by-product of those lessons.

Still, he felt compelled to defend what was indefensible.
"Anna, it's not my choice. I *have* to go."

In a hollow, toneless voice, "Of course you do. I heard.
Besides, you never meant to stay here forever."

And so it comes down to this, Zack thought with awful
clarity. He felt like someone had pulled the world out from
under his feet without warning. Even as he tried to identify
his emotions, his icy-sharp intellect was analyzing the black-
and-white facts. Without his being consciously aware of it,
or emotionally prepared, a decision had been made. The
only decision he felt qualified to make.

"I suppose we should be grateful for the timing," he told
her, his calm voice belying the bleak expression in his eyes.
"Just as Kyle and Carrie walk out the door, my life in Los
Angeles comes calling. If I'd been needed back any sooner,
we couldn't have pulled this off."

Anna was very, very still. Life teemed about them in the
small kitchen: the gauze curtains at the window billowing
with the morning breeze, the dishwasher humming, the
clock on the wall ticking away silent seconds. Three, two,
one...zero.

"Pulled it off?" she echoed dully.

Still he couldn't meet her eyes. "We made a good
team...that way."

"Made?" It seemed all she could do was parrot whatever
he said. Her fingers were shaking; she hid them away in her
skirts. She hadn't felt pain like this since...since forever.

Zack felt as if he had demons in his skull, each and every
one whacking away at him with a vicious little sledgeham-
mer. For Anna's sake, there could be no vacillation on his
part. The pain he was causing her now was at least finite—
there would be an end to it when enough time had passed.
The pain he would cause her if he tried to make her part of

his life permanently was infinite. He knew her generosity and courage. If he tried to explain his fears to her now, she wouldn't allow him to shut her out. She wouldn't understand the risk she was taking, not as he did. Damnation, why hadn't he been more careful at the beginning? He didn't mind the hurt he had caused himself. He deserved it. But the wounds in her pale face were unbearable to see.

"I suppose nothing lasts forever," Zack said. In this he lied. What he felt for her would last forever. He knew it as he knew the sun would rise in the east and set in the west. For a full minute, the communication between them took place in silence. It was the one thing he feared most in life—hurting those he cared about. "What happened between us...it wasn't planned. If I'd known...if I'd known..."

"What, Zack?" Anna asked ever so softly. For the first time since he met her, her eyes looked flat and completely lifeless. "If you'd known what was going to happen, if you'd known I was going to fall in love with you, would you have acted differently? Would you have let me go that first night and forgotten about me? Is that what you're trying to say? Are you feeling trapped now, like you don't quite know how to slip out the door?"

"It's not like that," he snapped. "That's not what happened with us, and you know it."

"What *did* happen with us? Explain it to me. Were we just playing another game?" She was looking at him in the way she would have looked at a total stranger. Warily. "It didn't feel like a game, but now I'm not so sure. Things get confusing at the end, don't you think?"

Zack took her hands in his. They felt cold to the touch, stiff and unresponsive. "You know damn well it wasn't a game. Anna, all my life I've tried to be honest. I've seen so much hurt stemming from people who refuse to face reality, who insist on ignoring their own flaws. I've known who I was and what my life would be like from the beginning. Do you know that the divorce rate among cops is higher than in any other profession? There are good reasons for that, believe me. I'm a good cop, a good friend and a very bad emotional risk. My father was a cop, and I'm his spitting image. The only way I can stop the chain of hurt that comes with my profession is not to involve anyone else.''

"Then," Anna said with sudden fire, "*that's* where you've failed."

"Failed?" Zack felt like he was losing his mind. He'd presented a brief, rational explanation. He'd explained how he felt, and it wasn't an easy thing to do. It was heroic, damn it. Anna obviously didn't get it. "I'm trying not to mess up your life any more than I already have. I'm looking out for *you,* Anna. My father never gave my mother that consideration."

Anna whipped her hands out of his. "Did your mother ever ask for that consideration?"

"Of course not. She didn't realize what was going to happen. She didn't know, not at the beginning."

"If you believe that, you're a fool." In that moment there was a clarity and maturity in Anna's eyes that Zack had never noticed before. "There's one thing I know about love, Zack. Real love. It takes away all your fear, giving you the ability to face anything. You're wrong if you think your mother didn't know from the beginning what life with your father would be like. She accepted it when she made the choice to love him unconditionally."

"You're not *getting* this, Anna. You didn't know my mother. And you sure as hell didn't know my father. His contributions to the world didn't include a shred of commitment to his marriage. Excuse me if I'm not willing to put you through something like that, let alone any children we might have."

"You made that clear when you said you knew who you were, and you accepted it. Well, *big double-damn deal!* We all know who we are. But some of us aren't willing to remain that way all our lives. Where you come from does not have to be where you end up, Zack. With all your experience in the cold, cruel world, you've never figured that out, have you?''

Zack's eyes were the color of clouds before a thunderstorm, dark and ominous. Somewhere in the back of his mind, his famous temper was stirring to life. "You don't seem to understand I'm making a sacrifice here! Because I love you.''

"You don't seem to understand that I'm not interested in your sacrifice," she shot back. "Moreover, I don't *need* it. Do you have any idea what would have happened to me if I'd accepted what life had handed me in the beginning? I'd be stuck in the 'chain of hurt' you talked about. But I waited and I hoped and I worked, and gradually it all came true for me. Even when my parents died, I refused to think my happiness went with them. I had their memories to keep me warm, I had my friends and my work. It would have been a lot easier just to give up, but I didn't. It's *always* easier to give up, but it's never right.''

"Don't tell me what's right and wrong," Zack bit out softly. "Do you think I want to walk out of your life?''

"*Yes.*" She was fast losing control, feeling tears stinging her eyes. The last thing she wanted right now was to let him see her cry. "Because that takes the pressure off you. You don't have to succeed where your father failed if you never make the effort. You don't have to prove once and for all what you're made of. It's so much easier to be a heroic cop than an ordinary human.''

Instinctively Zack reached for her, then let his hand drop to his side. She didn't want his touch, not now. And it seemed that the only gift within his power to give her was the gift of his absence. He hated himself for allowing her to be put in such a vulnerable position. It was thoughtless. It was cruel. It was just like something his father would have done.

"Anna...I'll always love you," he said haltingly.

"Don't. If loving me means you have to leave me, I'm not interested," she said coldly. "That kind of love is a little too conditional for my taste. Go home, Zack. And don't worry about me. I'll be fine, I really will. I always am."

"I know you will." Blind, unstrung to his soul, he turned on his heel and walked out of the room.

Ten

Men didn't like to go shopping. At least, men who were veterinarians didn't like to go shopping.

However, since Kyle and Carrie's wedding was only a few days away and the veterinarian didn't want to be sleeping on the sofa on his wedding night, he bowed to his lovely fiancée's wishes to act as chauffeur on her last-minute shopping trip with Anna. He had clear instructions to try to cheer Anna up whilst he drove the ladies hither and yon. He also had clear instructions to be sympathetic and not ask insensitive questions about Anna's abrupt breakup with Zack ten days earlier. He wasn't sure what might or might not be interpreted as sympathetic, so he played it safe by saying very little. Last but not least, he was sweetly asked not to wear his "favorite" shirt, a very loud green-and-red plaid that Carrie said would make a jolly Christmas place mat. This he could do with no problem. Lost in love and newly committed to be the perfect husband, Kyle just kept nodding his head at his beloved. Had she asked him if they could have twelve children, he would have just kept nodding. He had vowed to himself never to distress the love of his life again. He foresaw a smooth and unruffled existence together.

Tread softly, he thought. That was the ticket.

At the moment, the ladies were in the dressing room at Babette's Bridal Boutique, trying to choose a new bridesmaid's gown for Anna. The custom-made dress hanging ready in her closet was suddenly two sizes too big, and the seamstress had no free time to alter it until September. Carrie wasn't waiting until September to get married.

Kyle was seated near the dressing room, close enough to look attentive, but not so close that he would look like some sort of voyeur. He also kept his head politely averted, for fear he might get a glimpse of someone or something he shouldn't. He was taking no more chances. He was still shaken up by his near disaster. Never again would he look at another woman in *that way*. Except Carrie, of course.

A louvered door whooshed, then Carrie and Anna appeared before him.

"There's not a dress in the store that fits her," Carrie told her almost-husband, literally pulling at her hair. "I can't believe how much weight she's lost in ten days. Kyle, what do you think of this one?"

To look or not to look? Kyle wondered with a pang of uncertainty. As Carrie seemed to be waiting for his response, he reluctantly allowed his gaze to quickly skim over Anna from head to toe. He saw what was quickly becoming a familiar detached expression on her face. The blue sateen bridesmaid's dress wore her rather than the other way around, hanging limply on her shoulders, burying her breasts and not even pausing to consider her waist.

He realized with alarm that he had looked in the general vicinity of Anna's breasts. "A nice outfit," he gasped, focusing on a nearby rack of wedding veils. It was the least insensitive remark he could think of.

"Oh, dear," he said.

Carrie threw up her arms, completely exasperated. "It's not nice. This is the smallest size they have in this dress. Kyle, I'm at my wits' end. Anna, you simply *have* to eat yourself into this dress. We've got less than a week."

Anna smiled vaguely, patting Carrie on the shoulder. "Don't worry. I told you before, I think the other dress is just fine."

"Fine if you like curtains. You put Scarlett O'Hara to shame."

Kyle perked up at the mention of a new name. "Who is she, sweetheart?"

Carrie sighed. "You know. She's the heroine of...oh, never mind who she is. It's a good thing we're getting married, Kyle. You need to see more people and fewer animals."

"I need to see *you*," Kyle told her emphatically. "Every minute, every hour, every day. If I *didn't,* I doubt I would be sitting here in Babette's Bridal Boutique. It's a good thing I'm confident of my masculinity."

Momentarily distracted, Carrie gave him a private smile. "And so you should be."

Anna barely heard the intimate exchange. Her arms hung limply at her sides, listless and tired. She wasn't sleeping these days any more than she was eating. When Zack left her, he took her energy, her joy and her heart with him. Still, she was a fighter. She wouldn't let this make her bitter or resentful. Very thin, perhaps, but not bitter. If she knew then what she knew now...she would have loved him anyway. Heaven help her, that sounded like a country-western song. She winced at her maudlin train of thought.

"Are you all right?" Kyle asked quietly, catching her off guard. "You don't look so good, Anna." Belatedly he realized that was probably not a sympathetic remark, but he'd spoken only the truth. She hadn't been herself since the rat from California left her high and dry. If he'd had the time, he would have hunted Daniels down and given him a thrashing. *Not* having the time to spare was probably fortunate, given the size and build of said rat. "Anna? *Anna!*"

"Fine, I'm fine," Anna muttered, her wistful thoughts scattering like dead leaves in the wind. She hadn't realized Kyle had been speaking to her. Lately, he and Carrie had been caught up in themselves and their wedding plans, which was just fine with Anna. She hadn't told them much about Zack's departure, beyond a simple, "It didn't work out." Because her friends were busy with the arrangements for their wedding, they had very little time to dig deeper. Besides, Anna truly didn't know how something that had felt so perfect could have ended so badly. She'd been so certain that Zack had felt what she felt.

Unconditional love. It had turned out to be rather like a lush mirage in a scorched desert, a wishful fantasy that had disappeared under close inspection.

"You're too quiet," Carrie said.

"And *you're* overreacting." Anna gave her friend a pathetic imitation of her normally dazzling smile. "Not to worry, guys, I'm not about to spoil your big day. I'm a ray of sunshine."

"Does she look fine to you?" Carrie asked Kyle wryly.

Kyle took a moment to answer, fearing this might be a trick question. He didn't want his fiancée to misinterpret his concern for Anna. "Does she look fine to *you?*"

"She's had a sad hound-dog face for more than a week! Of course she doesn't look fine."

Kyle nodded. "That's exactly what I think. She doesn't look fine."

Carrie pinned her maid of honor down with a no-nonsense expression. "Anna, stop kidding yourself. Stop trying to kid *us*. You're not fine. If you'd just talk—"

"I do talk," Anna replied. "I talk all the time. Lately I've even been talking to myself, quite a bit, actually."

Carrie and Kyle exchanged a speaking look.

"Anna," Kyle said finally, "we're your friends. Friends can share anything, especially if there's a problem. It wasn't any secret how you felt about Zack. It was in your eyes every time he was in the same room. Unless I miss my guess, he seemed to feel the same."

"You missed your guess!" Anna said with brittle enthusiasm. "And now we're through talking. I appreciate you both more than I can say, but sometimes it's best just to let things alone. Besides, we've got a wedding to get ready for, so let's concentrate on that. I'm going to change into the other dress, Carrie. It's more formfitting, so it just might work."

With that, Anna and her blue tent went back in the dressing room. Carrie watched her with sad brown eyes, reaching out a hand to touch Kyle's shoulder. "She won't tell me a thing, Kyle. She's never been like this before, so closed up. She's hurting, and I can't help her."

"I knew he was a jerk the first time I saw him," the veterinarian said fiercely. "Daniels is a fool. I wished she'd never met him."

"I just wish I knew why everything blew up. All Anna will tell me is that he had to return to work in Los Angeles. I would do anything to help her. If I could just talk to him, maybe I could help. It could be that the whole thing is just a big misunderstanding."

"I think it's more serious than that," Kyle said gently. He hated to see the unhappiness on his beloved's face. And like any man in love, he wanted to make everything all right for her. "I feel so helpless. I wish there was something I could do."

"I wish there was, too," Carrie said wistfully. "I wish you could make everything all right." Then, with a shrug and a sad little smile, she trailed Anna back into the dressing room.

Because he was a normal man who was easily distracted, Kyle momentarily forgot Anna's sad situation while he appreciated the saucy sway of his fiancée's hips. Then, when she was out of sight, he turned his mind to the problem at hand.

I wish you could make everything all right.

The love of his life had spoken. Veterinarians might be poor shoppers, but given the right inspiration, they were certainly capable of heroics.

First came the invitation.

Zack grabbed the creamy white envelope from his mailbox as he dashed out to work. He barely glanced at it, then stuffed it into his pocket. Had Anna come custom-wrapped and delivered in his mailbox, he would have noticed. Anything else was invisible.

Later, when he and Pappy were in line at the drive-up window of McDonald's, he remembered the oversize envelope and took it out of his pocket. For the first time he saw the return address. It was postmarked Grayland Beach.

"What do you want?" Pappy said, interrupting Zack's sudden trance.

"Absolution," Zack muttered.

"Speak up, boy. What do you want to order? The usual?"

"What usual?" Zack snapped, throwing an impatient glance at his partner.

Clearly, Pappy didn't know what to make of the new Zack Daniels. Being a cop *without* emotional complications was one thing. Being a cop *with* emotional complications was another thing altogether. He had returned to Los Angeles in a black mood that appeared to be permanent. Everyone was spooked, even the irascible Captain Todd.

"Egg McMuffin?" Pappy cajoled. "You love those Egg McMuffins."

"I don't think I love Egg McMuffins anymore," Zack said. Actually, he didn't love much of anything these days. His job had lost its luster. He hadn't glanced at his portfolio once since he came back. He'd even gone so far as to turn off his pager when he wasn't working.

The thrill was gone. He had left it back in Grayland Beach, Oregon.

Logically he knew he had spared Anna the fallout from his demanding, high-risk, possible retirement-by-bullet profession. Unfortunately, he didn't feel heroic saving this particular damsel from distress. He felt lost.

Pappy was staring at him with one eyebrow heading for the sky. "The hell you say! As long as I've known you, you've been a McMuffin addict."

"I don't like McAnything these days. That was another Zack. Then I went to Appleton's for cold medicine, the fire door wouldn't open, and I played Candyland. My heart went out for a walk and never came back."

There was a baffled silence. "Are you crazy? What are you talking about?"

"You kind of had to be there," Zack said.

Pappy was a soft-spoken, gentle giant of a man with a heart as big as his impressive girth. He could tell his young friend was hurting, which in a way, absolutely stunned Pappy. He'd never known Zack to allow himself to care deeply about anything besides his job. He'd always wondered when the kid would realize he was just as human as anyone else.

Pappy whistled softly. "I don't believe it. You met someone."

"No. I met *the* someone. And I don't want to talk about it."

"Okay."

Zack glared at his partner. "What kind of friend are you? This is the place where you try and talk me into confiding in you. You're supposed to help me *vent*."

The soft-spoken, gentle giant got a teasing glint in his dark eyes. "I've never been able to talk you into anything. Still, I'll cooperate. Who is she?"

"Anna," Zack said softly, staring out the windshield at nothing. The single word held a wealth of feeling.

Pappy stared at the ivory envelope in Zack's hand. "Is that from her?"

"No. I think it's a wedding invitation from some friends of hers I met." Zack opened the envelope and skimmed the formal script. "The pleasure of your company..."

"Are you going?" Pappy asked. "Obviously it's a chance to see her again, and you don't seem too happy to be back here in your old stomping grounds."

"I couldn't bear to tear myself away from work," Zack said dully. A verse in bold print at the bottom of the invitation caught his eye.

On this day
I marry
my dearest friend.

"I think I don't want to talk anymore," he said quietly. "For real this time."

"You love her?" his partner asked. "If you love her, what's the problem?"

Zack had a sudden flashback of Pappy's wife, Paula, in the emergency room when Pappy was shot. The agony, the uncertainty, the stark fear in her face were all things he would never forget. In that moment probably every nightmare she had ever had about the consequences of her husband's work had come true. He'd seen a paler imitation of that look on his own mother's face every time his father was late coming home from work. "The problem is what we do, Pappy. The problem is who we are. I chose my course a long time ago. You and Paula—somehow you've made it work, but that doesn't make it any easier on her. Or on your children. How do you do it? How did you decide it was all worth the price your family pays?"

Pappy sighed heavily, and for once the customary good

humor was absent from his face. When he finally spoke, his soft, deep voice was powerful in its simple conviction. "That wasn't my choice to make. It was hers, and I respected it. Women who love men like us, who give us children and stability and a warm welcome home when we finally trudge in the door at night…they're the heroes, Zack. They're the reason we can do what we do."

Zack wished desperately he believed that. There was a darkness inside him, missing her. He felt as if he didn't belong to his custom-made life any longer. He'd gone away for his vacation, and when he'd come back, all the rules were changed on him.

"I don't know what's right anymore," he said softly.

When Zack returned home that evening, yet another surprise awaited. A really big one.

Kyle was sitting on his front porch in a little plastic lawn chair he'd apparently dragged around from the backyard. His arms were crossed, his eyes were hard, and he wore the ugliest red-and-green shirt Zack had ever seen in his life.

He could only think of one reason for Kyle's visit. "What's happened? Is Anna all right?"

"Nice little place you've got here. Lawn needs mowing, though." Then, with a slightly different tone in his voice, Kyle added, "She's fine. Anna's a fighter. She'll survive you just like she survived everything else in her life. And what's more, she'll come out on top."

Zack sighed heavily, sinking down on the front steps. He realized the irritating veterinarian spoke the truth. "Thank you for sharing that with me, Kyle. For what it's worth, you couldn't possibly make me feel worse than I already do."

"Let's make this simple," Kyle said. "I've got a wedding coming up, and I don't have any time to waste. Do you love her?"

Zack stared at him. For whatever reason, he dispensed with sarcasm, evasion and pride. "Yes."

"Then why are you here while she's in Grayland Beach?"

"*Because* I love her. How did you find me?"

"Remember good old Frank, the judge? I knew you worked somewhere in Los Angeles, he did the rest." Kyle let out his breath in a soft sound. He decided to lay it on the line…just as Zack had done when Kyle had taken a turn at being a raving lunatic. "I thought you were very unimpressive when I first met you, but I never thought you were stupid…until you left Anna high and dry. To me, that is the rationale of a stupid man."

"Actually, I'm a genius," Zack said dully.

"Sure you are." Kyle stood up, pushing his hands in his pockets. Now he was a great deal taller than Zack, which he liked. "Do you remember what you told *me?* To quote, Anna isn't responsible for this mess. You turned schizo on her. You're an idiot, and—"

"I never called you an idiot. Not to your face."

"Be quiet, I'm not through! How could you take a woman like Anna for granted? She is funny, bright, beautiful, everything a man could want." Kyle paused, a smug smile tipping his lips. "Anything sound familiar, good buddy?"

"You've never seen my temper yet," Zack said with deceptive mildness. "Believe me, you don't want to get me going."

"Oh, like I'm scared of you? Last night I assisted a Doberman pinscher giving birth to thirteen puppies. Nothing can scare me after that." Kyle started pacing the length of the porch, moving swiftly and impatiently. This was the closest he got to ever losing *his* temper.

"What do you think, I'm made of stone? I didn't just meet Anna, I fell in love with her. And living without her is killing me. There. Are you satisfied, Doolittle?"

Kyle's brow furrowed. "Doolittle? Oh. Very funny. Look, I was only apart from Carrie for a couple of days and

I went berserk. Why are you putting yourself through this? More importantly—why are you putting Anna through it? What went wrong between you two?''

"She's not talking?"

"Not a word. At least, not about you."

Zack took a long time to answer. His head hurt. His heart hurt. What did a true hero do in a situation like this? Especially when the heroine had been hurt too much and too often, long before she met him. All the lines he had drawn in the past were blurred, all the convictions fading fast.

What did a true hero do?

Zack realized with something akin to awe that his breathing was quick and frightened. *Rope's end,* he thought. *That's where I am.*

He looked over his shoulder at the visiting veterinarian. "I've got some beer in the fridge. You want to come in? I need a friend."

Eleven

The countdown was at three days. Three days until Kyle and Carrie were married. Three days until they left on their honeymoon and gave Anna a little peace. Three days until Anna could drop the stiff-upper-lip act and allow herself to grieve.

Zack had never even given them a chance. That's what hurt the most. When she thought about it, which was constantly, she got an actual physical pain in her chest, as if her heart had literally been broken. It was there, crushing her, all the time.

Five years from now, Anna thought, I'll look back on this experience and think, *What a good lesson I learned from that. I'm a much stronger person now.*

But that healthy perspective was five long years away.

Carrie called first thing that morning, uncharacteristically babbling about having second thoughts—not about her wedding, but about her wedding dress.

"It's wrong," she told Anna, sounding tearful. "Wrong,

wrong, wrong. When Kyle sees it, he's going to hate it. Hate, hate, hate.''

"Are you going to be *in* it when Kyle sees it?"

"Yes…''

"Then he won't hate it," Anna said impatiently. "Carrie, I've got the bath running, and I need to—''

"We've got to do something," Carrie said in a breathless rush. "Today. I want to make sure there's nothing else in town I'd like better.''

"There's nothing else in town you haven't already tried on." Her cool and calm friend was being unusually emotional, Anna thought. Maybe the wedding was giving her a few jitters. "Just calm down, eat something with lots of sugar and call Kyle and tell him you love him. You'll feel much better, and I won't have to trail behind you to every store in a fifty-mile radius all day, only to realize you like your original dress best. Yes?''

"No," Carrie said stubbornly. "Anna, you have to come. I have water-weight buildup and I'm all puffy and swollen. Especially my waist. I can't decide if a dress is pretty if I can't even get into it. You can try on the dresses, and I can stand back and get a good look. See? You *have* to come with me.''

"You're losing it, Carrie," Anna said.

"This is the time when my best friend should support me and indulge me. I'll be over to get you in forty-five minutes." *Click.*

Anna had very little interest in what she looked like lately. Consequently, she took a great deal of care getting ready. This was how she had always gotten through her problems, to face the worst of them square on and refuse to buckle in. If she *acted* like she was normal, she would eventually *feel* normal. Hopefully.

She applied a bit more makeup than usual, then slipped into a simple white sheath dress that set off her complexion beautifully. Then she twisted her long hair into a glossy knot on the top of her head, put on chunky silver earrings and the delicate silver bracelet that had played such an important part the night she had first met Zack. She wanted to look the opposite of the way she felt. She wanted to appear composed, elegant, happy and content. In reality, she was coming unglued, had no desire to wear anything but her old ratty terry-cloth bathrobe and could hardly remember what it had felt like to look forward to anything. Happiness had left town with the romantic policeman.

And then it was off to Babette's Bridal Boutique once again.

"Why here?" Anna asked Carrie, following her friend through, around and between the racks of frothy white bridal dresses. "You've been here three times already. You've got to have all the merchandise memorized by now."

"Stop whining," Carrie said. "This is a lovely store, and they have a bigger selection of dresses than anywhere else." She sorted through a rack of dresses, pulling out four in quick unison. "Here," she said, shoving them at Anna. "They're all your size. Try on each and every one. And *don't* forget to come out and let me see them all. And save the strapless beaded satin for last. I have a feeling that one will look the best on you. On me, I mean."

Rolling her eyes, Anna trudged off to the spacious dressing rooms to fulfill her maid-of-honor duty. That was her job, after all, to make sure she assisted the bride in any way possible.

The trouble was, she truly didn't want to try on wedding gowns. She didn't want to see herself in the mirror, didn't want to imagine what Zack would think of her in the dress. But it seemed like lately fate didn't really care what Anna Smith wanted.

Dresses one and two were dismissed as too plain. Dress three was, according to Carrie, like a white birthday cake with too much frosting. Icky. Anna went back to the dressing room like an obedient robot and tried on the last dress, the strapless beaded satin that seemed to be Carrie's favorite.

It was amazing.

Anna's big blue eyes seemed to take up half her face as she stared at her reflection in the dressing-room mirror. Her lower lip trembled ever so slightly, reacting to the sudden pitch and drop of her heart in her chest. It might have been designed particularly for her coloring, the rich ivory satin setting off her luminous skin and gleaming tawny hair. Her creamy shoulders were bare above the simply cut strapless bodice. The beaded material was nipped in at the waist, then draped over her hips with an elegant, narrow skirt. A fairy godmother couldn't have improved upon the whole. The dress wasn't Carrie's style at all, but oh, it worked magic for Anna Smith.

She closed her eyes, blinking away the tears that threatened. When she opened them again, Zack Daniels was standing in the dressing room behind her.

"A candy necklace would be a perfect touch," he said.

Anna couldn't speak. She couldn't breathe. She just stood there in her beautiful dress, her eyes locked with his in the mirror. It's not real, she thought. *But what if it is?*

"What are you doing here?" she asked hoarsely.

Zack was also having trouble breathing. When he'd opened the dressing-room door and seen her in that dress, he'd received a mortal wound to his heavy-duty, double-insulated cop heart. Desire rushed through him like the hard current of a wild ocean wave. Never had there been a more beautiful woman in the world. Never had there been a more beautiful wedding gown in the world. Put the two together and not a man in the world could have resisted. Had Zack seen her for the first time at this moment, he would have loved her at first sight.

Then again, he *had* loved her at first sight.

"I couldn't wait for you to come out of the dressing

room,'' he said, the words hurting his tense, arid throat. ''I wanted to see if I was right.''

Anna turned to face him, her palms touching the heat in her cheeks. She could hardly take him in—the ebony hair, silver eyes, casual jeans and shirt that didn't begin to disguise his own brand of smooth, dark elegance. ''Right about what?''

''About the dress. Babette met me here at ten o'clock last night and I picked it out myself. The minute I saw it, I knew you would break hearts in that wedding gown.''

Anna blinked, shaking her head dazedly. ''Are you crazy, or am I?''

Zack took a step closer, bringing him near enough to Anna to smell her perfume. He took a deep breath and drank it in, his heart running wild with ecstasy and fear…a humbling and powerful cocktail of all-too-human emotions. The pure love he felt for her was so intense, his soul seemed to ache with it. He had never known he was capable of this depth of feeling. ''Kyle came and saw me a couple of weeks ago. We talked, we argued, we talked some more…and finally I realized something.''

''What?'' she whispered. She had lost her battle with the tears, but she hardly noticed.

''I need rescuing, Anna.'' His heart was in his eyes. For the first time in his life, he hid absolutely nothing. It was an immense relief to finally admit it. ''I figured I was born to *do* the rescuing, but I was wrong. I thought you needed protecting, but I was wrong about that, too. You're the strongest woman I have ever known in my life. I knew that, but I guess I needed some perspective to really understand.''

Anna's thick lashes worked to clear her vision. Her heart was slamming into her ribs, wreaking havoc on her breathing. ''Understand what? You seemed pretty clear on what you wanted—and didn't want—when you left. What could possibly be left to say?''

He swallowed hard, then cleared his throat. This was the

moment he had anticipated and wanted and dreaded and prayed for on the flight to Oregon. It was the reason he had taken six aspirin in a futile attempt to calm his nerves. He'd had three Bloody Marys for the same reason, with the same result. Nothing had tamed his anxiety.

Anna's eyes went round as he dropped to one knee. Rounder still when he pulled a small velvet box from his pocket and flipped it open.

"Please rescue me," he whispered. Everything was shaking, his fingers, the ring box, his voice. "I'm lost, Anna. It's like I ended when we ended. I love you so much. Marry me, Anna. Just trust me one more time, and I swear I'll never let you down again."

Anna stared at him. "You left me," she whispered.

Zack's lips twisted painfully. "I thought I was saving you from my life. Then I realized I had no life without you. I don't know how we'll solve it all or how hard it will be or where we'll live. But if we're together...we'll be all right."

Babette's Bridal Boutique had an enormous grandfather clock ticking away in the front of the store. Suddenly it began to chime, one...two...three...all the way to twelve. The silence that followed was surreal. Twelve o'clock, the all-important hour in fairy tales. Anna felt as though someone had cast a spell over her, rendering her unable to speak or move. "Yes," she said in a tight whisper.

Zack's pulse was no longer measured in beats. It had quickened into a waterfall, strong and wild. *Yes* was the only word he had wanted to hear. But he needed to hear it more than once.

"On Saturday," he said hoarsely. "Three days from now. Will you?"

"What? Zack, I can't. You know Carrie and Kyle are..."

"Looking forward to a double wedding. Believe it or not, Kyle's agreed to be my best man. God must have a wonderful sense of humor." Zack's smile felt shaky, his eyes hot and stinging. "Anna, say yes and I'll never knowingly

give you cause to cry again. I know this is just the beginning
for us, but I promise to do whatever it takes to make you
happy and keep you safe. Please…. Wear this dress and
walk down the aisle to me and teach me how to believe in
forever.''

"Three days?" Anna breathed, her eyes softly unfocused.
"Oh, my."

"And…one more thing." A pause, then with a tinge of
guilt to his voice, "I probably should tell you about my
financial circumstances. I'm not exactly what you would call
a wealthy man."

"You think that matters? Zack, I don't care if we have
to struggle, as long as—"

"No, you don't understand." He cleared his throat. "I'm
not a rich man, Anna. I'm an obscenely, jaw-droppingly,
filthy-rich man. I sort of have a way with stocks, and…I
ended up with all kinds of money. Like…*lots*. We couldn't
spend it all in one lifetime."

Too many surprises, Anna thought, sinking down on the
padded love seat in the corner. Too much to take in all at
once. "I don't know what to say."

"Just tell me you'll marry me in three days." His eyes
reflected all the love and promise in the world. "Sweetheart,
my knees are killing me, but I'm not getting up until you
say yes."

A soft, slow smile came to her face, sunshine after rain,
hope eclipsing despair. "Yes," she said unsteadily.

The single, heartfelt word signaled the end of Anna's tenuous control. With a gasp she slid off the love seat, going
down to the love of her life like hot wax. Never had Babette's Bridal Boutique seen such unbridled enthusiasm in
its clientele. Caught between laughter and tears, they kissed
in mad, lost ways, shaken, hungry and elated. They were
too joy-filled to be eloquent, too desperate to worry about
propriety. They had come so very close to losing it all.

And that was how Babette herself found them a moment

later, wrapped in each other's arms and kissing shamelessly right there on the lavender carpet in the dressing room. Shock lifted the woman's ample bosom at this public display of affection, then she sighed, and an envious smile tipped her lips. Without Zack or Anna being the wiser, she carefully tiptoed out of the dressing room.

It looked to be the beginning of a very happy ending.

Epilogue

"**W**e don't need to have a really *large* family," Anna said. "Maybe five. Would that be all right with you?"

Zack's head turned slowly, gauging her seriousness. "Five?"

They were sitting on the porch swing, waiting out a rainstorm on the wraparound porch of the Victorian. Since discovering she was pregnant four months earlier, Zack's wife was nesting for all she was worth. Ferociously.

"And it's good to have them close, don't you think?" Anna said innocently, setting the porch swing to rocking with her bare foot. "So they'll all be best friends."

Zack smiled faintly, touching her rounded stomach with his hand. "Can we concentrate on this one? I'm still in the nervous daddy stage. What if we have a girl and she gets herself a boyfriend that we *know* is going to be trouble—"

Anna grinned, tucking her head into his shoulder. "Then you can take him out to your boys' ranch and get him sorted out. Isn't that why you founded it in the first place? Think how convenient.''

Since marrying Anna, Zack had discovered there were more ways to make a difference in the world than just being a cop. His fortune had gone to good use, building a sprawling ranch in the foothills east of Grayland Beach for troubled teens. Surprisingly, he'd found his new undertaking every bit as challenging as being a cop and far more rewarding. The story didn't end on a hopeless note when he put someone in jail. He was able to follow the kids through their hard times, get them counseling and provide some sort of family atmosphere that they had usually lacked in their own homes. In three years the ranch had earned an excellent reputation.

Anna had been the one who had come up with the idea in the first place. It would be a wonderful way to put the ''pots and pots'' of money he had brought into their marriage to good use. Plus it would give them the opportunity to work together. Anna identified with the kids who came to the ranch, particularly teens who had a similar background to her own. Not only was she a good teacher, but at times she was a better counselor than the counselors.

''Nothing fazes you,'' Zack said. ''I'm really glad you're in this baby thing with me. You can be the calm, logical mother, and I'll just panic right and left. Kind of like a good cop, bad cop thing with a twist. Good mommy, nervous daddy.''

''I'm kind of glad you're in this baby thing, too.'' Anna laughed. ''I would have had a terrible time doing it without you. Besides, you underestimate yourself. You're wonderful with the boys you work with, and you know it. And you'll be wonderful with the baby, too.''

Zack smiled down at her, loving her with his soft eyes. In his heart, he was at peace. Somehow, like orphans in the storm, they had found each other. He never looked at his wife without giving thanks to someone far more knowing and powerful than himself.

"What about as a husband?" he asked softly, kissing the tip of her nose. "How am I doing there?"

"You're perfect. Usually."

"Usually?"

"I'm not one to complain, but that kiss was a little...tame. But sweet."

He still loved challenges. He did much better this time, pressing a long, openmouthed kiss on her lips that left her dizzy. "How's that?"

Anna wriggled in his arms, finding the porch swing a little cramped. "Improving *vastly*. Maybe if we changed the location...?"

Zack consulted his watch. "It's almost 8:00 p.m.," he said. "Don't you think it's late? You should be in bed. Pregnant mommies need lots and lots of sleep."

She pulled a face. "Zack Daniels, if you think I'm going to sleep—"

"Trust me, sweetheart."

And Zack Daniels, husband extraordinaire, took it from there.

* * * * *

Silhouette Desire

presents

DYNASTIES: THE CONNELLYS

A brand-new miniseries about the Connellys of Chicago,
a wealthy, powerful American family tied by blood to the
royal family of the island kingdom of Altaria.
They're wealthy, powerful and rocked by
scandal, betrayal…and passion!

Look for a whole year of glamorous and
utterly romantic tales in 2002:

January: **TALL, DARK & ROYAL by Leanne Banks**

February: **MATERNALLY YOURS by Kathie DeNosky**

March: **THE SHEIKH TAKES A BRIDE by Caroline Cross**

April: **THE SEAL'S SURRENDER by Maureen Child**

May: **PLAIN JANE & DOCTOR DAD by Kate Little**

June: **AND THE WINNER GETS…MARRIED! by Metsy Hingle**

July: **THE ROYAL & THE RUNAWAY BRIDE by Kathryn Jensen**

August: **HIS E-MAIL ORDER WIFE by Kristi Gold**

September: **THE SECRET BABY BOND by Cindy Gerard**

October: **CINDERELLA'S CONVENIENT HUSBAND
by Katherine Garbera**

November: **EXPECTING…AND IN DANGER by Eileen Wilks**

December: **CHEROKEE MARRIAGE DARE
by Sheri WhiteFeather**

Silhouette®
Where love comes alive™

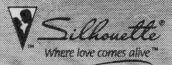

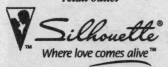

Three bold, irresistible men.
Three brand-new romances by today's top authors...
Summer never seemed hotter!

Sheiks of Summer

*Available in August
at your favorite
retail outlet!*

"The Sheik's Virgin" by Susan Mallery
He was the brazen stranger who chaperoned innocent, beautiful
Phoebe Carson around his native land. But what would Phoebe do when
she discovered her suitor was none other than Prince Nasri Mazin—
and he had seduction on his mind?

"Sheikh of Ice" by Alexandra Sellers
She came in search of adventure—and discovered passion in the arms
of tall, dark and handsome Hadi al Hajar. But once Kate Drummond
succumbed to Hadi's powerful touch, would she succeed in
taming his hard heart?

"Kismet" by Fiona Brand
A star-crossed love affair and a stormy night combined to bring
Laine Abernathy into Sheik Xavier Kalil Al Jahir's world. Now, as she
took cover in her rugged rescuer's home, Lily wondered if it was her
destiny to fall in love with the mesmerizing sheik....

Silhouette®
Where love comes alive™

Visit Silhouette at www.eHarlequin.com   PSSOS

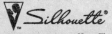

**Where royalty and romance
go hand in hand...**

The series continues in Silhouette Romance
with these unforgettable novels:

HER ROYAL HUSBAND
by Cara Colter
on sale July 2002 (SR #1600)

THE PRINCESS HAS AMNESIA!
by Patricia Thayer
on sale August 2002 (SR #1606)

SEARCHING FOR HER PRINCE
by Karen Rose Smith
on sale September 2002 (SR #1612)

And look for more Crown and Glory stories in
SILHOUETTE DESIRE starting in October 2002!

Available at your favorite retail outlet.

COMING NEXT MONTH

#1453 BECKETT'S CINDERELLA—Dixie Browning
Man of the Month/Beckett's Fortune
Experience had taught Liza Chandler not to trust handsome men with money. Then unbelievably sexy Beckett Jones strolled into her life and set her pulse racing. Liza couldn't deny that he seemed to be winning the battle for her body, but would he also win her heart?

#1454 HIS E-MAIL ORDER WIFE—Kristi Gold
Dynasties: The Connellys
Tycoon Drew Connelly was unprepared for the sizzling attraction between him and Kristina Simmons, the curvaceous bride his daughter and grandmother had picked for him from an Internet site. Though he didn't intend to marry her, his efforts to persuade Kristina of that fact backfired. But her warmth and beauty tempted him, and soon he found himself yearning to claim her....

#1455 FALLING FOR THE ENEMY—Shawna Delacorte
Paige Bradford thought millionaire Bryce Lexington was responsible for her father's misfortune, and she vowed to prove it—by infiltrating his company. But she didn't expect that her sworn enemy's intoxicating kisses would make her dizzy with desire. Was Bryce really a ruthless shark, or was he the sexy and honorable man she'd been searching for all her life?

#1456 MILLIONAIRE COP & MOM-TO-BE—Charlotte Hughes
When wealthy cop Neil Logan discovered that beautiful Katie Jones was alone and pregnant, he proposed a marriage of convenience. But make-believe romance soon turned to real passion, and Neil found himself falling for his lovely bride. Somehow, he had to show Katie that he could love, honor and cherish her—forever!

#1457 COWBOY BOSS—Kathie DeNosky
Cowboy Cooper Adams was furious when an elderly matchmaker hired Faith Broderick as his housekeeper without his permission—and then stranded them on his remote ranch. Cooper didn't have time for romance, yet he had to admit that lovely Faith aroused primitive stirrings, and promoting her from employee to wife would be far too easy to do....

#1458 DESPERADO DAD—Linda Conrad
A good man was proving hard to find for Randi Cullen. Then FBI agent Manuel Sanchez appeared and turned her world upside down. He proposed a marriage of convenience so he could keep his cover, and Randi happily accepted. But Randi was tired of being a virgin, so she had to find a way to convince Manuel that she truly wanted to be his wife—in *every* way!

SDCNM0702